MAXIMUM LIGHT

Also by Nancy Kress

NOVELS
The Prince of Morning Bells
The White Pipes
The Golden Grove
An Alien Light
Brain Rose
Beggars in Spain
Beggars and Choosers
Oaths and Miracles
Beggars Ride

STORY COLLECTIONS
Trinity and Other Stories
The Aliens of Earth

MAXIMUM LIGHT

NANCY
KRESS

A TOM DOHERTY ASSOCIATES BOOK/NEW YORK

This is a work of fiction. All the characters and events portrayed in this novel are either fictitious or are used fictitiously.

MAXIMUM LIGHT

This book is printed on acid-free paper.

Edited by David G. Hartwell

Designed by Basha Zapatka

A Tor Book
Published by Tom Doherty Associates, Inc.
175 Fifth Avenue
New York, NY 10010

Tor Books on the World Wide Web:
http://www.tor.com

Tor® is a registered trademark of Tom Doherty Associates, Inc.

Library of Congress Cataloging-in-Publication Data

Kress, Nancy.
    Maximum light / Nancy Kress. —1st ed.
      p.   cm.
    "A Tom Doherty Associates book."
    ISBN 0-312-86535-X (acid-free paper)
    I. Title.
PS3561.R46M39   1998
813'.54—dc21   97-29850
                                         CIP

First Edition: January 1998

Printed in the United States of America

0 9 8 7 6 5 4 3 2 1

For Charles, sitting and talking and wrangling

For all we have and are,
For all our children's fate,
Stand up and take the war.
                    —Rudyard Kipling

The gods
Visit the sins of the fathers upon the children.
                    —Euripides

MAXIMUM
LIGHT

1

SHANA WALDERS

By the time they truck us to the staging area, which is the parking lot of some old church, the train has been burning for two days. It's one of those new Korean maglevs that isn't supposed to derail ever, no matter what, but there it is in some D.C. suburb, burning like a son-of-a-bitch. Carrying some sort of fuel canisters; somebody says that it could burn for a week if the scientist-types don't figure out what to do. Which I guess they haven't, because the area is evacuated and glow-marked, and we jump off the truck a couple thousand feet away from the wreck. Other trucks are bringing in civvies, some of them crying.

"You have entered an area electronically cordoned by the United States Army," the truck is saying over and over. "Unless you are authorized to be in this area, turn around immediately and leave. You have entered an area electronically—" My NS sergeant reaches into the cab and slaps it off. She goes to report in to a regular-army sergeant, so I sort of slouch over to a soldier and say, "On. What we got?"

He gives me that look they all do, the *Who-let-you-put-on-a-uniform-and-by-the-way-you're-not-real-army-anyway-asshole* look. But I ignore that and repeat, "What we got here?" and this time I smile at him, the just-a-hint-of-promise smile, and he don't resist. They never do. I'm a gorgeous kid.

"We're taking the evacuees back in, in twos. For their pets."

"Their *pets?*"

"Yeah, sweetheart. The army's just one compassionate subrun." He laughs, but I don't get the joke. They got a lot of jokes like that, the regulars do, to keep us NSs on the outside. I don't care. We're going in.

"Got your adrenalin up, huh?" the soldier says. "Your little titties erect?" They're not supposed to talk like that to us—such fragile youngsters like us, just doing the year of National Service we owe our country—but I don't care. I can handle soldiers. And my titties are anything but little.

I laugh, and the soldier moves closer. His eyes gleam. He isn't that old, and not bad looking, but I'm not in the mood. We're going *in.*

"Shana," my sergeant calls, "over here. You and Joe hand out gear, help the civilians put it on. Send them by twos over there."

"On. You aren't keeping me *here*, are you?" I say. "Instead of going in?"

The sergeant sighs. They handle us with velvet gloves in the NS, not like at all like the rough stuff in the real army. We're a precious resource, after all, us kids. Fewer of us every year, what with the fertility crisis. It's all right by me. I smile at my sergeant. *That* smile.

"Oh, all right, you can go in," she says. "But first get some of these people in gear. Fall to."

I fall to, shouting at Joe to bring over two civvies, pulling two hazard suits off the back of the supply truck. The civilians are old, of course, but not real feeble fusties, probably no more than fifty. They climb into the suits with no trouble. The woman, though, don't want to put the helmet on.

A lot of people are like that, scared to seal off their heads. Even some NSs. She stands with her gray hair—she don't dye it, God knows why not, I sure would—blowing into her eyes, which are red and swollen.

"It's my cat," she says, almost like she's apologizing to me. "Widdy. Short for Kitty-Widdy, embarrassing as that is." She smiles at me, almost begging. For what? I don't know her cat from dogshit.

"Please put on the helmet, ma'am," I say. I'm getting a real kick out of sounding in charge, even if I'm really not.

"When I left the house to go shopping, Widdy only had a little water left in her bowl," the woman pleads. "And that was two days ago!"

"Yes, ma'am. Please put on the helmet."

"I was out *shopping*. I wasn't even at home when the train derailed!"

"Yes, ma'am. The helmet, ma'am."

"I . . . can't."

"Then please remove your suit, ma'am, so someone else can wear it to rescue their pet." I'm making this up as I go along. I love it.

"I . . . can't. What about Widdy?" She looks wildly around, like maybe there's somebody else to go rescue Widdy. I guess she don't see nobody, because suddenly she jams the helmet over her head. I reach out and seal it for her. Behind the faceplate, she's crying.

I hope I never get that scared of life.

I point toward the regular army, and she shuffles off in that direction. Joe and I pull two more sets of gear off the truck and the sergeant sends another two civvies shuffling toward us. This time they *are* moldy oldies, barely strong enough to pull on the damn suits. All around the church parking lot, NS teams are suiting up civvies. I watch carefully, the whole procedure, to be sure I know how to work it so I actually get sent in. I'm holding my sergeant to her promise.

Hanging over the parking lot is a huge holosign with the usual government garbage: SHARED RESPONSIBILITY: TOGETHER WE STAND. Shimmery holo people of all different ages, holding hands and smiling at each other like morons. Suddenly thick clouds of black smoke blow in our direction, blotting out the sign. I don't put on my helmet unless I absolutely have to—I'd rather soak it all in undigitalized—but for a moment I can't see the signs, the trucks, the civvies, the fancy stained-glass window in the front of the church, with its blue and red figures of some ancient saints older than rocks. The smell is awful—like burning tires mixed with rotted garbage. Then the wind shifts and the smoke blows in the other direction.

I don't get to go in until afternoon. They let the regular army do it for hours, truckload after truckload of civvies, probably to be sure it's safe for us precious little NSs. Us kids have to do a year of National Service to learn selfless dedication to the good of the group, blah blah, but nobody wants us to get killed. By noon, when nobody's been blown up and the eight regular soldiers are due for rotating breaks, they let us have a turn. I'm right there with the first bunch.

I'm paired with a soldier who, behind his faceplate, looks in his forties or fifties, a career soldier, all business. We jump in the back of a truck with eighteen suited, scared civvies all thinking about their dogs and cats and parakeets. The truck rumbles along toward the burning wreck.

The soldier briefs me. "Nobody goes in closer than eight hundred feet. Nobody. This lot swore they all lived farther away than that, but they could be lying. You escort your charge in and out of the house. They get four minutes, you time it. Grab the pet and out. Nothing else, this is just about pets. If they can't grab their animal in four minutes, out anyway. By force, if you have to. They even teach you kids to use your stun gun?"

"Yes, sir," I say, ignoring the insult.

"Just the pets," he repeats. "No money, pictures, terminals, furniture, jewelry. And don't fucking get yourself injured."

"No, sir." I flash him a big smile. He stares at me a minute, then looks away, his mouth twisted in disgust. I don't care. I'm too damn happy.

The smoke gets worse, and pretty soon we can see flames. That train is burning like the hell the preacher used to try to tell us about, when I was in the government school. Another glow marker, waist high, with the field set to bright yellow, snakes along eight hundred feet from the maglev track. The houses beyond the marker are standing, all right, but I wouldn't bet much on that if any fuel canisters blew. What *is* that stuff, anyway? Probably some long unpronounceable name only stewdees would care about.

We stop about a hundred feet from the marker. Eighteen civvies, three soldiers, three NSs. The sergeant gets the first six civvies off the truck and running toward houses, each civvy with a soldier or NS. Some of the civvies could barely shamble along. My civvy is never going to win any marathons, but he moves pretty fast for a mosstooth. I trot along beside him, parallel to the marker glow. Other pairs disappear into the smoke in other directions, or into houses, which are the little row-jobbies you get in places like this. I see one soldier-with-civvy come out almost immediately, followed by a big dog barking its fool head off with doggie joy.

We trot on. And on. Where does this guy live? We're almost at the end of the houses. Beyond are just big gray windowless buildings, warehouses or factories or something. There wouldn't be any pets in those. Would there?

All of a sudden the civvy puts on a big burst of speed. Son of a bitch! He's away from me before I can get out my stun gun, which I hadn't been expecting to even need. Not to rescue a fucking kitty! The mosstooth races away from me and right through the glow marker. When I follow him through, there's a brief burst of pain in my chest, but nothing my suit can't handle. We're inside the explosion zone. I'm gaining on him, but not by much, when he runs into the nearest big gray building.

And locks the door behind him.

I waste precious seconds pounding on it like some kind of stewdee. Then I run around the outside of the building. In the back is a loading dock, but it's locked, too. So is the emergency exit. How come these people had time to lock everything up tighter than a religious virgin?

Then I see my guy running out of a little side door. He don't expect to see *me*, clearly, since he almost runs into me. Which is how I get a good look at what he's carrying in his arms.

And I don't even *draw* my stun gun. I'm the one stunned. It's like I can't even move.

Until I realize what's going to happen next. *Has to be.* The guy has already disappeared into the smoke—he knows where he's going, all right, and how much time he has to get there. I don't. But I start running for everything I'm worth, away from the windowless building, and every second I'm farther away is a gift, a present, a fucking miracle. Another second I'm alive.

The building blows.

I dive behind somebody's brick barbecue—by this time I'm back among the houses—and crawl inside. It's got a metal cover to keep rain off the grill, because the grill is jammed with terra cotta dishes and wooden spoons and shit for cooking. The terra cotta shatters and rains down on me, but otherwise I'm okay. I cover my head and wait and, sure enough, the building explosion ignites the closest of the train cars and it blows, too.

Poisons. Toxins. Radiation? What *is* the stuff in those canisters?

I don't know and it wouldn't help me if I did. I'm screaming my throat raw until I notice and make myself stop it. The noise all around me is like the end of the world. The black smoke makes it impossible to see my own knees, even though I'm crouched so that my face is jammed up against them. I'm pretty sure I'm going to die. If all the train cars blow, I'm probably going to die.

But they don't, and I don't.

From the sound, only one car ignites, and I ran away from that direction. I can't remember if I ran back through the glow marker, out of the explosion zone. I didn't feel no marker. I don't feel nothing for a few more minutes, except the fact that I'm fucking *alive*. Then I crawl out of the barbecue pit and stand, wobbly.

My helmet switched itself to virtual vision, for better resolution. Around me it looks like a war movie, something from the action in South America. Houses burning, houses fallen down. The gray building just isn't there no more. Only rubble, and smoke, and noise that rings in my ears like it was far away instead of practically on top of me.

I wobble my way between the fires and back toward the staging area. Somewhere I've lost my direction because I approach the church parking lot sideways, from between two houses on its east side.

The parking lot don't even look real.

Old people everywhere, some still in suits without helmets, some out of suits, everybody smeared with soot so you can't tell if they're black or white or purple. And pets. A dead cat lying on the pavement, with a woman wailing over it, tears streaming through the wrinkles on her face. A live puppy, one foot crushed but wagging its tail like Christmas morning, while another rusty fusty cries over *it*. A big Labrador retriever racing around in circles, barking and barking. Cats spitting at the Lab. Vets with medical scanners crouching over dogs. A geezer holding an empty dog dish, just standing there gazing at it, never moving a muscle. The regular army soldiers trying to load the civvies back onto trucks: "It's not safe here, sir. Get on the truck immediately. Leave the dead animal, please—"

Nobody listens. Vid crews maneuver their robocams, people wail and shout. And closest to my side of the parking lot, a huge sooty parrot digs wicked claws into the shoulder of a grinning man who don't even wince, the bird squawking over and over, "Access granted. Here we go! Access granted. *Here* we go! Access granted—" And in the distance but coming closer, the scream of more fire-fighters and equipment arriving by air.

My sergeant spots me. She's crossing the parking lot at

double time, and she glimpses me between the buildings and stops dead. Her face changes completely, and I know what I'm looking at. Relief. She thought I was dead, and that she was the one who lost a precious NS, and that she would have to pay for that real hard and real long. Only here I am, alive. Never mind that no civvy isn't with me—the civvy isn't nineteen years old and a national resource.

"Walders!" she snaps at me, and I know just how upset-relieved she is. Usually they call us by our first names. "Report in!"

And I do. I wobble forward, on knees made of water, and not because I almost died. Not because I lost my civvy, either, and fucked up the first hazardous-duty NS assignment I ever got. My knees wobble because I have to report in, a full report, including exactly what I saw the running civvy carry away with him. And I don't know, can't even imagine, what will happen to me after that.

2

NICK CLEMENTI

It's the same dream. I sit beside my mother by the duck pond, throwing our lunch to the ducks. "See, Nicky, the babies swimming behind their mommies! If we were duckies, you'd swim right behind me and Jennifer and Allen." "I want to swim in front of Jen'ver and Allen!" I say, and my mother laughs. She is very young herself, and beautiful, sitting barefoot on the grass. The ducks fight over the bits of peanut-butter-and-jelly, and quack and shrill and shriek and become my wrister.

I rolled over in bed and said, "Reception."

"A call, Dr. Clementi," said the MedCenter computer in its pleasant, androgynous voice. "Code Four. Mrs. Paula Schaeffer. Complaints are tingling in left leg, lethargy, irritability. Instructions, please?"

"Schedule a visit in the morning," I said, probably as irritably as the would-be patient. If the computer decided the call was a Code Four, it could wait. Tingling in the leg could be anything, was probably nothing. Lethargy, irritability—Mrs. Schaeffer always had those, as far as I could see. She was eighty-seven years old, for God's sake, and it was two o'clock in the morning. Did she expect to be dancing a jig and planning a party? But they were all afraid everything meant a stroke.

The wrister had woken Maggie. "Nick? Do you have to go out?"

"No. Just another Fretful Fossil." Our private name for them—even though we ourselves were both in our mid-seventies. Or maybe because. Joke about it, taste it, get used to it in small silly references to other people, and it will be easier to live with. *Mithridates, he died old.*

Maggie rolled to nestle, spoon-fashion, against my back. Buttons on her nightdress poked into my skin.

"Your clothing is attacking me again."

"Sorry, love." She shifted position.

"Not good enough. Take it off."

"You're a dirty old man, Nick." And then, "Nick?"

It was going to be a good one, a hard one. I could feel it.

She was light and sweet in my arms. In her forties and fifties Maggie had gained weight, a hot exciting cushion underneath me, but in her sixties and seventies it had all come off again, and I could feel her delicate bones. And that fragrance—Maggie always had a fragrance to her, a unique odor, when she was ready. She was ready now. Her thin arms tightened around me, and I slid in, and it was indeed one of the good ones.

"Oh, nice, nice," Maggie said, as she had said for fifty-one years now.

"I love you, Maggie."

"Uhmmmmmmm . . . oh, yes, Nick, just like that."

She always knew what she wanted. For fifty-one years, I've been grateful it was me.

Afterward, the wrister rang again. Maggie dozed, one leg flung over mine, a stray white curl tickling my nose. I must have slept, too; morning light filtered through the curtains. Maggie woke and shifted. "Damn it, why can't they let you sleep? Don't answer it; it's probably just a tingling in Paula Schaeffer's other leg."

"Unlike what's tingling on you," I teased.

"Don't answer it, Nick."

"Reception," I said to the wrister.

"Probably a tingling in Paula Schaeffer's eyelashes."

But it wasn't. It was Jan Suleiman, clerk for the Committee, and a long-time friend. Often Jan made sure I heard things some people would prefer I not hear. I listened, and slowly sat up, staring into the darkness across our bedroom.

"Nick?" Maggie said. "What is it?"

When the call was finished, I told her. I always told Maggie everything, even things I should not. She was absolutely trustworthy. I told her about my remaining patients, about the economic struggles of the Doctors for Humanity Volunteer MedCenter, about the political struggles at the Congressional Advisory Committee for Medical Crises. There was only one thing I hadn't told her yet, and I would, when the time was right. So now I repeated to her what had been allegedly seen yesterday, in the maglev explosion northeast of the city, in Lanham. Then I held her for a long minute before getting up, and dressing, and calling a car for the ride from Bethesda to the Hill.

The permanent Congressional Advisory Committee for Medical Crises met in an anonymous and unpretentious office building. There were good reasons for this. First, there were so many Congressional Advisory Committees in these days of perpetual crisis that the government buildings were always full of anxious huddles of legislators, scientists, lobbyists, military officers, bureaucrats, toxicologists, industrialists, educators, doctors, economists, and activists. But an anonymous office building was also less likely to be watched by the press, whose involvement would be premature at this point. Everybody thought so, except me. I thought the press was long overdue.

Still, I could see the other committee members' point: much of the press still dealt in inflammation and hysteria, especially about the aftermath of the Tipping Point. They had a lot to answer for, although they probably never will.

But the main reason for the anonymous office building was the secret tunnel system from the anonymous parking garage two blocks away.

They built for secrecy a decade ago, when they could afford to build at all. Well, they had to. It was right in the middle of the Tipping Point, when the looming financial crisis of the US government wasn't merely looming any more, and the slow worldwide decline in viable sperm suddenly wasn't slow anymore, and the backlash against genetic engineering weren't just theoretical anymore, and the coming bankruptcy of elderly entitlements wasn't just coming anymore: it was all here. Along with the riots and the tax rebellions and the genetic laws and the entire destructive chaos of the Tipping Point, those two painful years before the president used martial law to restore order. A lot of otherwise unreticent people don't say what they did during those two years. In Washington, some of them used secret tunnels to do it.

A few blocks before the parking garage, I saw the child. This wasn't a good part of Washington, which had so few good parts left. Litter blew between the buildings, some of which had burned down, more of which were boarded up. The May night had been mild, and old people slept on sidewalks and fire escapes and in doorways, wrapped in coats and blankets. It was a city of the elderly—like practically every other city.

One in four Americans was over seventy. There were only 1.4 taxpaying workers to support each "retiree," even with the wretched non-living-level subsidies most elderly received. The number of "very senior citizens," those over eighty-five, had quadrupled in the last fifty years. The global birthrate was less than twenty percent of what it had been a century ago. In some countries it had dropped to five percent. In the relative absence of children, the world had grown old.

We drove past the huddled sleeping forms. Past the holosigns, the most visible aspect of Project Patriot, bright cavorting shadows whose captions urged SHARED RESPONSIBILITY and THE SOCIAL CONTRACT = YOUR GUARANTEE OF A GOOD FUTURE! Past the broken bottles and drug discards and human shit—the usual. Plus, of course, the rats, bolder and more aggressive than rats had ever been in the entire history of man. I knew why, but the committee wouldn't let me tell them.

And in the middle of the early-morning street, dressed only in a pink tunic, a brown-skinned toddler with huge dark eyes and long black hair topped with a crisp pink ribbon.

"Stop the car," I said to the driver, who was already screeching to a halt, as startled as I was. This did not happen. Washington was at the bottom of America's regional variation curves in sperm count—the bottom for motility *and* normalcy *and* volume—and thus for birth rate. Artificial conception, in all its varieties, was still too expensive for most couples, now that the health insurance industry had crashed. And cloning, which had once seemed the hope of the world, had turned into a bitter joke.

You could clone worms, frogs, sheep, elephants. But not humans. A cloned, unfertilized human egg obediently divided five times, into thirty-two cells. And then it went on dividing, instead of first gastrulating in the first of the many crucial folds that lead to cell differentiation. In cloned eggs, no cell differentiation occurred. Ever. You ended up not with bone cells and skin cells and muscle cells but with a monstrous ball of cells all the same, the homogenous mass growing more and more huge until somebody killed it. Researchers attributed this to subtle disruption of the embryo's chemical polarity gradients, although nobody had yet figured out the exact mechanism. They only knew the results. Cloning could not provide the infants the world craved.

And so children were scarce and precious; they were not allowed to turn up half-naked and alone in the middle of filthy streets. Especially not children with no visible birth defects. There were a great many infertile couples who would kill for this little girl.

She looked up at me without fear, and put two fingers in her mouth.

"Hello," I said, through the powered-down window. Beside me, the driver drew his gun. Children as bait were not unknown to the truly desperate. "What's your name?"

"Rosaria," she said around the two fingers, and started to cry. I got out of the car.

"Why are you crying, Rosaria?"

"Abuela didn't dress me." She lifted the edge of her

tunic to show me her naked legs and genitals. Hastily I pushed the cloth back down again. If this got caught on robocam . . . HILL SCIENTIST CAUGHT MOLESTING CHILD.

"Where's Abuela now, Rosaria?"

She pointed down a side street. The driver said, "Sir . . . I can call Child Protection. . . ."

"Do that. And the cops." But meanwhile Rosaria was tugging on my hand and crying. "Rosaria, we have to wait for some people to come before we find Abuela."

"Abuela fall on the floor!"

I was a doctor. I went with her.

She led me a short way down the nearest side street. SHARE RESPONSIBILITY advised the building graffiti, along with FUCK RESPONSIBILITY! My driver stayed behind, talking on his wrister. I held the child's small hand as we climbed filthy, crumbling steps, through an apartment-house door half off its hinges, up a flight of stairs reeking of garlic and despair. The staircase wasn't equipped with even common reinforced railings and non-skid treads, let alone the aid-summoning sensory monitors that were guardian angels to the elderly rich. At the top of the stairs were three apartment doors, one wide open. Inside, an elderly Hispanic woman lay on the clean floor, between two carefully darned chairs that had once been bright red. One look at her and I knew I was too late. Myocardial infarction, or burst aneurysm, or any of a dozen other causes of death common to the very old. In her hand she held Rosaria's pink tights.

I knelt before the child. "Rosaria . . . Abuela's dead. She's not in that body anymore. Do you understand?"

She nodded, although of course she couldn't understand. But she had stopped crying. Her big dark eyes were

very soft, like the fur of black kittens. From behind the red
chair she plucked a Grandma Ann doll, one of the toys distributed as part of Project Patriot. The young must be
taught early to embrace the old. Rosaria clutched the doll
tightly.

"Sweetheart, who else lives with—"

"Aaeeehhhaaaeeee!" A cry of anguish from a huge Hispanic woman hurtling through the door. "Abuelita! Aaeee-
hhhaaaeee!"

I stood up and stepped back.

The woman, who looked in only her early twenties, col-
lapsed beside her dead grandmother and began wailing.
She wore factory coveralls, stitched DONOVAN ELECTRONICS.
After a few moments, I put a hand on her shoulder.
"Ma'am . . ."

To my surprise, she leapt up from the body and whirled
on me.

"Who you? What you doing here?"

"I'm a doctor. I found Rosaria wandering in the street;
she said her abuela had been dressing her. . . ."

"In the street? You took her in the *street*?"

"No, I . . . she came out by herself. After your grandmother—great-grandmother?—collapsed, I   presume.
I was—"

"You wasn't doing nothing! You hear me? We're just
fine without no Child Protection!"

"I'm not from Child Protection. I—"

"You just leave us alone!"

She took a step toward me. Her eyes blazed with hatred.
She was as tall as I was, twenty pounds heavier, and fifty
years younger. I stepped back.

"I find somebody else to watch my Rosaria. You ain't

going to take her away to give to some rich bitch whose husband's balls empty and whose test-tube fucking don't take. Bad enough I got to work two jobs to support you old white farts, you ain't getting my child too!"

"Ma'am, you are—" I was going to say, *blocking my pathway to the door.* I don't know what she thought I was going to say. Her face suddenly crinkled horribly and she swung on me. Caught off balance, I went down, wildly thrusting out my left hand to arrest my fall. My fingers slammed into the floor. I felt two of them break.

Only one punch. She stood there, panting, horror at what she'd just done creeping slowly into her eyes, while Rosaria wailed and neighbors boiled into the hall and the scream of police flyers approached outside.

We looked at each other across the din—of noise, of my hand, of her dead grandmother who was Rosaria's sole caregiver, of her desperate fight to keep and care for her child from the affluent so hungry for it. Affluent for the most part as white as the old people this woman subsidized with nearly fifty percent of her paycheck. The essentially bankrupt government protected children, but did not fund day care. Kids should be cared for by their families, was the national mood. That was the responsible way. And if families couldn't, or wouldn't, care for their children—then give the kids to the rich white couples panting for them.

Still on the floor, I examined my fingers. Although I couldn't be sure without an X ray, I guessed they were simple fractures. The siren stopped outside. I said softly, "Pick up Rosaria. And let me go tell the cops everything is under control."

She did. Out of fear, or hope, or maybe just not knowing what else to do. She stepped aside and picked up her daughter, who buried her head in her mother's neck and clung hard. I pushed past the scowling neighbors to greet the police, letting my hand dangle casually as if nothing were wrong with it, planning how to tell the cops there was a body here but no foul play. How to tell the Child Protection that, yes, Rosaria had no one to raise her while her overworked, overtaxed mother put in six ten-hour factory shifts a week because she needed the overtime—but that everything was under control, nothing here needed official intervention.

Everything was just fine.

3

CAMERON ATULI

There are only forty-two people in the world, and I know all of them.

Nobody looks at me any differently as I hurry from the boys' wing through the corridors of Aldani House, late again to morning class. "Say," Nathan calls, perky even at this hour, damn his beautiful eyes. Melita nods formally: "Good morning, Cameron." Shoes in hand, I fly pass Yong and Belissa, who smile. I might never have been away. I might never have had significant portions of my brain deliberately, selectively, expensively walled away.

What was in those memories? *You will ask yourself a thousand thousand times*, Dr. Newell told me, her gray curls bobbing, *and each time will be the first.*

"Cameron," Rebecca, our ballet mistress, says severely as I rush to my place at the barre. "We would have been thrilled to see you fifteen minutes ago."

"I'm sorry," I say, and resist the impulse to add, *What do you expect of a delete brain?* What Rebecca expects is for everyone to be on time at her class, or at least everyone in the company who's currently dancing. Thirty-one dancers. I take my place at the barre.

"Plié," Rebecca calls. "And one and two and . . ."

Thirty-one dancers, including the students in the Aldani School who are too young to join the company officially.

Plus Rebecca, Dr. Newell, my nurses Anna and Saul, Aldani House security technician Yong, Nathan and Joe and Belissa on staff, and Melita, our business manager. And of course Mr C., artistic director and choreographer, who's famous all over the world. Forty-two, in all. Everyone in the whole world.

Who else lived in those deleted memories? *You will ask yourself a thousand thousand times.*

"Left side," Rebecca calls. "And one and two . . ."

I've missed warm-up, and my muscles are cold. I take the barre exercises in half-time until my muscles warm. The main practice room at Aldani House is long and narrow, lined with barres and mirrors on both sides. On the shorter south wall, open windows overlook the front gardens. Delicious fragrances drift inside: roses and lilac and other flowers that would be wonderful to gaze on if Rebecca ever gave us a second to look at them. She doesn't.

"*Battement tondu* . . . good, good . . . now into the *adage* . . . Sarah, don't distort your hip line, keep the turn-out . . . Joaquim, higher. *Higher!*"

I have been away for two months, back for one. That's what they told me. You can't be away from dancing for three months without losing some technique. But I am flexible and strong, and the technique is returning. I can feel it.

I am twenty-two years old. My name is Cameron Atuli. What could I have done, or been done to, that I would elect memory deletion? And that Aldani House, perpetually stretching its endowed budget, would pay for it?

My body gives me no clues, except . . . but I don't want

to think about that. And anyway I don't really want to know why my memory was wiped. I can still dance. Nothing else matters.

The first dream comes a few days later, early in the morning just before I wake. I am running, pumping my legs as fast as I can, so scared I can't see straight. Something is chasing me. I can feel it draw closer, closer. I stumble, and turn around, arms thrown up to shield my face. I can hear myself screaming. And what leaps on me is . . . a cat. A pet kitty, licking my arm and purring while I cower and scream. I wake in terror.

Is this a memory? Did I have a pet cat, once? But memories from before the operation aren't supposed to be able to get through to me, none of them. And why would I be so afraid of a memory of a pet cat?

I lie in bed alone, shivering. And why am I in bed alone, anyway? Did I have a lover, before? Who?

I speak three languages. English, French, some Cajun. How do I know these languages? The answer—all the personal answers from before my operation—are blocked forever from my conscious access. All "autobiographical memory retrieval" is coordinated by something called the Gereon node, in the right temporal cortex. My Gereon node has been "deactivated."

I remember factual knowledge (Two plus two is four; Gerard Michael Combes is president; Aldani House is named for its founder and endower, a billionaire who loved ballet). Skills, too, are all there. I can speak, read, dance, because apparently those things are stored in a different way in my brain. What we have given you, the doctors said, is an induced retrograde amnesia—a sort of Alzheimer's in reverse. I don't know what Alzheimer's is but I don't really care. I can still dance, and perhaps one of the boys in the company will become my lover.

The dream can't hurt me.

I spring out of bed and stretch. It feels good, it feels wonderful. Today I'll do an extra barre. We're rehearsing *Prodigal Son;* I'm dancing the lead. I'll do my barre next to Rob, who is quiet and gentle, with marvelously expressive arm movements. He also has beautiful blue eyes.

I pull on my practice clothes and go down to the kitchen for coffee.

We are doing *grands battements* at the barre when I smile at Rob. Rebecca is not in a very good mood this morning, and she snaps out the combinations: *front, back side, plié. Repeat. Turn.* During the turn Rob smiles back at me, a little uncertain, very appealing. Playfully, I touch my extended leg to his ass. Rebecca notices—she notices everything, she runs a very good class—and yells at me. "Cameron! Stay in place!"

I am in my place. I am happy.

"Would you like to go for a walk?" I say to Rob, after class. He has slung a towel around his neck, the same blue as his eyes. Sweat mats his hair and darkens his practice clothes. He nods, smiling.

We clatter down the back stairs and out into the garden of Aldani House. The area inside its nine-foot foamcast wall is about four acres. I don't know how I know this. The main building sits close to the front gate, which is just as solid and high and opaque as the wall. Between the House and the gate bloom the front gardens; off to one side are a security building for Yong and the maintenance sheds. Behind the House are a stretch of lawn with plastic tables and chairs and a volleyball net, then the vegetable garden where the School's small pupils are sent to work when they misbehave, and then a little wood with paths and benches and thickly leaved trees. Rob and I walk there. The air is cool on my warmed muscles, and the air smells of pine needles and cherry blossoms and strawberries.

"You have a beautiful *porte de bras* in your arabesques," I say. "Much more expressive than mine. I was watching you in the mirror."

"But you can jump," Rob says. It's true. I have the strongest and most precise jumps in the company.

We stroll through the wood until we come to a clearing beside the wall. Against the foamcast, which is made to look like rough stone, stands an unpainted wooden bench. Without talking about it, Rob and I sit.

I reach down and pluck a wild strawberry. It tastes warm from the sun, sweet and juicy. Rob looks at me oddly.

"What?" I say.

"Nothing." He gazes away. But I guess what his look means: *You didn't use to like strawberries.* I'm getting used to this look. Apparently many of my tastes were different before the operation. Then, people tell me, I never wore purple; now I love it. Then I listened every day to Ragliev; now I refer the classical composers, especially Schubert. Then I wore rings and bracelets and vest pins; now a pile of jewelry sits gathering dust on my messy dresser top.

The silence stretches out. To break it, Rob says, "Look at that poor bird." It's a sparrow, hopping on the ground on its one foot. There's also something wrong with the shape of its wings. I remember that there are a lot of deformed birds.

The bird flies awkwardly away. I eat another strawberry. More silence. Rob and I don't look at each other. When I can't stand it anymore, I put one hand on the rough wall. "What's on the other side?"

He turns to blink at me. "You don't remember the city?"

I shake my head, smiling at him. His eyes are so blue.

"Not anything about this particular neighborhood?"

"No," I say, and for the first time, I realize that of course Rob knows what happened to me to send me to the memory doctors. Everyone in Aldani House must know; only something terrible enough to be general knowledge would justify the operation. Why haven't I realized this before? I draw away from Rob, confused and suddenly ashamed. These people don't just remember me with different tastes; they possess crucial pieces of my life that I don't have.

Rob blurts, "Don't push me away, Cam! Not again! When you smiled at me in class this morning, I thought, I hoped . . . don't push me away again!"

Again. The word makes me uneasy; he knows so much about me. Rob sees my reaction and puts his hand on my arm. "I'm sorry, I'm not supposed to do that. Don't worry, none of us will ever talk to you about what happened to you . . . before. Nobody, ever. Mr. C. and Melita were both very clear about that. And we love you, Cam, you must feel that. I . . . love you."

I say, despite my uneasiness, "*Were* we lovers? Before?"

He doesn't answer. I think again about the one part of me that feels somehow different since I've returned . . . although I don't even know what I mean by "different." Just different in my hand when I shower, or masturbate. But everything still functions just fine, so what difference could any difference really make?

I repeat, "Were we lovers? Before?"

"Yes," Rob whispers. And then, "But this is now. I know that. Melita warned me that . . . This is now, and you're starting over. I'm just . . . glad you're here with me now, like this." He makes a tremendous effort; I can see him doing it. Gathering himself together, as if for a *flick jeté*. He says lightly, "What's on the other side of the wall is a city street, with some expensive houses and very nice shops. We can go there tomorrow, if you like."

I say, before I know I'm going to, "I'm not going to leave Aldani House."

His eyes widen. "Not ever?"

"No." I feel safe here.

"But . . . but you have to dance outside, you know. You're a principal dancer. The company leaves on tour next month!"

On tour. I taste the idea. On tour would mean moving from place to place with most of the company, or at least a good chunk of it. Sarah and Dmitri and Caroline and Joaquim. Plus Yong to protect us and Melita to organize everything and Rebecca to conduct class, just as if we were all still home. . . . Dancing every night in front of strangers, but on a stage, separated from the audience out there unseen in the dark. Yes, I can do that. I nod. "Of course. I'm dancing *Prodigal Son*."

Rob relaxes. "Well, good. And you don't have to go to any shops outside if you don't want to. Although there is a bracelet in Jewel of the Ages there that would look so good against your skin . . . yum."

Shyly he holds his arm parallel to mine. His skin is pale, milky beside my richer light brown. And it's back, the smiling and gaze averting and eye widening. The electricity. I don't mention that I no longer wear bracelets. However, Rob won't initiate anything, because I don't remember the past and he's a sweet and considerate man. All at once a surge of happiness floods through me, pure pleasure that feels familiar even though I don't remember it. I laugh, and lean over, and kiss Rob on each blue, blue eye.

His arms slide around me. We kiss there on the bench, beside the rough wall and under the budding trees, and I think how lucky I am to have had a memory operation and so have the chance to discover him for the first time all over again.

4

SHANA WALDERS

The committee that advises Congress don't meet in the Capitol building, like I thought. Instead the federal marshall escorts me to an office building that looks like every other office building in downtown D.C. Foamcast-and-glass. A few sickly trees out front, looking like too many homeless peed on them. The usual signs about social responsibility, except these are carved into the building instead of being holos. Lots of railings, non-skid floors, medical field-monitors—more safety than class.

The committee room don't have much class neither. Wood tables and chairs, cloth curtains at the windows, china coffee cups, a dinky three-foot flat screen—you'd think important people like that would do better for themselves. None of the stuff you see on vid: flashy wall programming or window opaquers or holoscreens or those cups that dissolve themselves when the drink's gone. Maybe this isn't such an important committee after all, and maybe my report isn't so important neither. But then why did they bring me in person, instead of just vidding what I have to say? And the very next day after the train car exploded? And escorted by a federal marshall?

I'm important. Bet your betty bytes on it.

"Private Walders?" the committee leader says. "Thank you for coming. Sit there, please."

I sit, straight and tall. He's a moldy oldie, of course, but sharp-eyed. He don't smile. More people drift into the room, get coffee, make small talk. Seven men, five women. I'm the only one under fifty except for a cowed-looking man in the corner. The women wear suits with the pants cut full, business style, and their vests are brighter than the men's. I'm in National Service full dress uniform. Introductions get made: Congresswoman This, Doctor That. Centers for Disease Control. Federal Drug Administration. Pharmaceutical Manufacturers' Association. National Sperm Bank Task Force. Child Protection Agency. More, but I stop trying to remember them.

On.

"Private Walders, please tell this committee your birth date."

Not what I expect. What the fuck does it matter when I was born? I'm here to say what I saw. But I answer crisply, like a soldier. "November fourteenth, 2015, sir."

"And you are nineteen?"

"Yes, sir." He can do math. Congrats.

"How long have you been in the National Service Corps?"

"Ten months and thirteen days, sir."

"In what division?"

"Army Adjunct, sir." He can tell that from my uniform. Like I'd choose Environment Reclamation, or Project Patriot, or any of those stewdee divisions. Since I owe my country a year of responsibility, why wouldn't I want it to include some action?

"And you did your orientation where?"

"Pittsburgh, Pennsylvania. Sir."

Now a woman takes over; I forget what agency she's from. She studies a data readout on her wrister. "Private

Walders, could you describe your official record in National Service thus far?"

Uh-oh.

I say, "My official record contains one commendation and seven reprimands, ma'am."

Her eyebrows go up. Bitch. "*Seven* reprimands? In ten months? For what?"

"The commendation was for excellence in physical training," I say, even though she didn't ask. "The reprimands were for various offenses against Service standards."

"Detail them, please, Private Walders."

"Yes, ma'am." I hold onto my temper. I'm going to play this by the book, no matter what. "Three for violating curfew, two for lying to a superior, one for starting a fist fight during official training exercises, and one for inappropriate conduct while in uniform."

"Lying, twice?" Her eyebrows go even higher. If she knew how stupid she looked, she wouldn't do that. "What did you lie about? Detail each occasion, please."

"The first time, about the curfew violation. The second time, about having returned my weapon to Stores."

The committee chairman takes back over. "If I may, Dr. Janson. Private Walders, I understand that you hope to eventually join the regular army."

"Yes, sir."

"I served in the army, well before you were two cells in your mama's womb." He smiles; I don't. My heart is beating too fast. It's not that easy no more to get into the regular army. With modern weapons, they don't need too many soldiers. They're picky. If these fuckers wreck my chances . . .

"Your seven violations, innocent-sounding enough in

the terminology of National Service Corps, carry other language in the regular army. You were AWOL. You perjured yourself during an official reprimand. You struck a superior officer. You were guilty of conduct unbecoming. And you stole a Class III government-issue weapon."

"I didn't steal it, I just didn't turn it back in at exercise debriefing! And it was only a stun gun!"

He rolls on like I didn't say nothing. "Now, in the army, any of those actions would earn you a discharge. Are you aware of that, Private Walders?"

If I say yes, he'll take me apart as an untrustworthy fuck. If I say no, he can easily show that I'm lying—the base library in Pittsburgh has records of my studying every dee-bee I could access about the regular army, including the discharge regulations. I don't say nothing, sitting as tall as I can, looking straight ahead. The silence goes on, and on, and the son-of-a-bitch lets it. Now all the old mosteeth are studying their wristers—with my record on it. I feel like I can't breathe right. Just when I think I can't stand this one more second, the door opens.

"I'm sorry I'm late, Mr. Chairman, ladies and gentlemen. Private Walders? So sorry to distract from your testimony. There was a car accident. No, no, it's nothing, just superficial."

He's the oldest person here, and his left hand has one of those little casts foamed around two fingers. I could of kissed the cast. Everybody forgets me and puts their attention on his accident. Murmurs, questions, so-sorry's. Finally, real sour, the chairman gets everybody back to business and introduces my rescuer to me. These people would be polite at a cat-burning.

"Private Walders, this is Dr. Nicholas Clementi, Nielson

Institute Director Emeritus, and advisor on vivifacture to
this committee. Dr. Clementi, we have just been establish-
ing Private Walders's . . . credibility."

And my Service record flashes up on the wall screen.

Dr. Clementi glances at it, then at my face. The shit-
eating chairman is about to start in on me again, but
Clementi cuts him off. "I see. But I'm afraid my time here
is limited this morning, Mr. Chairman—*my* doctor's orders"—he touches his cast with his right hand and makes
a little face—"so with your permission, I'd like to move
right to the part of Private Walders's testimony that I'm
qualified to remark on."

I *will* kiss him, I swear it. Chairman Fucker scowls but
don't argue. This Dr. Clementi must be really important. I
try to look like a credit to my country.

"Private Walders, I'm a little confused about what happened during the train wreck in Lanham. Wasn't the regular army directing the evacuation? Can you tell me how
your National Service cadre happened to get involved?"

He's giving me a chance to tell it my way. I do, helped by
a few questions from him. I explain about the pet rescue,
and how there'd been nobody hurt for two solid days, and
I throw in a little grease about how a few of us outstanding
NSs were being given the chance to use our physical training in a way that provided genuine assistance to the army,
blah blah. He keeps his eyes on me the whole time. For a
rusty fusty, he's all right.

"So you then ran around to the back of the building to
try to find a way to follow your assigned civilian inside?
That was brave."

Now he's greasing me, but that's okay. "Yes, sir. And
every door I had time to try was also locked tighter than . . .

was locked tight. Then I see the civvy run out of another, little door alongside of the building. He don't expect to see me, I don't think, because he runs almost into me before he looks real startled and swerves away."

Chairman Fucker says, "Presumably providing you with a perfect chance to intercept him, since you've said you were so set on doing that. Did you draw your stun gun, Private Walders?"

"No, sir."

"Why not?" It's like a left cross.

"I was caught by surprise, sir. I didn't expect to see him, and I—"

"Somehow that seems at odds with your supposed excellence in physical training."

"— and I was just completely shocked by what he was carrying."

"Allegedly carrying," some woman says, but at the same minute Dr. Clementi says, "And what was he carrying?" Which lets me ignore the bitch. *Allegedly*, my ass.

"He was carrying a cage, sir. One of those super-light plastic cages with e-locks, with the bars so thin they're barely there." Meaning, *I got a good view*.

"And what was in the cage, Private Walders?"

I take a deep breath. This is it. Everybody here already knows what I'm going to say—I figured out that much, at least, by how they're trying to make me look like a liar— but it's my big moment anyway. I planned on playing it out for all it's worth, but now that the time is finally here, something else happens. I'm just swamped by the memory itself. Those hands . . . those feet . . . a shudder runs through me, and I hear my own voice, not dramatic at all, even a little weak and sick:

"In the cage was three monkeys, sir. With . . . with human faces and hands."

"I see," Dr. Clementi says, like he might actually believe me. "Did they look like this? It's a computer drawing based on your report to the NS. Please tell us how accurate it is, to the best of your recollection."

A picture flashes on the screen. And it's dead accurate.

Three chimps, crowded into the cage. Hairy monkey bodies, long dangling arms, those long feet that can curl around the bottom bars of the cage. Hands clutching the side bars, faces peering out. But the faces are all the same face, and it's human. A child, with smooth light-brown skin and big hazel eyes flecked with gold. Lips molded firm and sweet—in fifteen years he'll be prime stud-meat. Right now he's the most adorable toddler I ever seen—except he's a monkey. Or she is. One of three toddlers is a girl. Only they're not toddlers—they're *monkeys*. With the same human face and chubby pink-nailed hands, but different hair. One has shiny straight black hair, one has blond curls, one has red fuzz. I see that on the drawing the redhead has a light dusting of freckles. Yeah, that's right—I told that to my sergeant, and again to the captain who vidded my statement.

"Yes, sir," I say, and I hate that my voice wobbles a little. "That's what I saw."

"Except that it's impossible," the bitchy woman said. "Dr. Clementi, setting aside the fact that any tinkering with germ-line human genetics is completely forbidden since the Tipping Point legislation—aside from that, and in your professional opinion, does any scientific community anywhere in the world possess the expertise to create this sort of human-chimpanzee genetic hybrid?"

"No," Clementi says.

"To come even close to creating such a hybrid?"

"No."

"And you're absolutely positive about this?"

"Completely. Even countries in which genetic engineering is allowed are decades from creating anything like that. The problems seem insuperable." Like cloned human eggs, cross-species engineered DNA divides to thirty eggs and then fails to differentiate.

The congresswoman smirks. "Then you're saying that Private Walders couldn't possibly have seen what she claims she saw."

"No," Clementi says. "I didn't say that."

"I don't understand."

"Dr. Clementi is prepared to explain," the chairman said, "but not just yet. There are matters of security involved." And he glances toward me like I'm some kind of security risk.

I can't help it; the blood rushes to my face. Fuck them, fuck them all.

Clementi steps in again. "Before we get to my testimony, I'd like to ask Private Walders a few more questions. You've been very helpful, Private Walders, and your reporting your experience to your sergeant was a patriotic act. Tell me, did you realize that what you saw must be radically against the law?"

"Of course, sir."

"You knew that the stiffest possible mandatory penalties attach to even trying to create any kind of animal-human crossbreed?"

"Yes, sir." Although didn't he just say that wasn't possible anyhow? I'm getting confused.

"And you knew from your previous experiences that any more lying to your superiors would probably end your chances of being accepted in the regular army, after your Army Adjunct Division National Service was over?"

"Yes, sir." My sergeant told me just that, in her strongest words, which were pretty fucking strong. And she must of told the Committee that she told me.

Clementi says, "How badly do you want to join the army, Private Walders?"

"More than anything in the world, sir. My father was army. I don't know who he was, but I know that much. Mom told me before she died."

"So is it fair to say that you have absolutely no motive to lie to the NS, or to this committee, about what you saw? In fact, finding out that you *did* lie would wreck your chances of getting your heart's desire?"

"Sir, I am not lying. *I am not lying.*"

The chairman was scowling. "Dr. Clementi, I'm afraid we have a bit of misunderstanding here. You were asked to join us in order to share your scientific expertise, not to establish a subpoenaed witness's motives and credibility. The committee requests you to confine yourself to your own scientific area. Do you have any more descriptive questions to ask Private Walders?"

"No, I do not."

"Fine. Then, Private Walders, the marshall will escort you back to your NS base. He will also explain to you your obligation to repeat nothing you heard in this room, and the penalties for any violation of that obligation."

"I wouldn't—"

"Thank you, Private Walders."

The federal marshall stands next to my elbow. I stand up,

my face hot, and tell myself to leave quietly. They're a Congressional committee, for chrissake—big shots. There's more power in this room than I'll probably ever talk to again. I should leave quietly, not say nothing else, just leave even if I'm boiling over inside. . . .

I can't do it. At the doorway I turn back. "If you old farts do anything to fuck up my chances of going regular army, you'll regret it. Every one of you. No matter how long it takes me!"

From his seat Clementi shakes his head at me, but it's too late. The marshall grabs my arm and hauls me out of the room. But not before I see the smirk on the bitch who was riding me. She got what she wanted: proof that I'm an unrestrained disrespectful hothead nobody should never listen to. And I *gave* that to her, damn it all to fuck. . . .

I just screwed myself.

5

NICK CLEMENTI

By the time I arrived at the advisory committee meeting, the battle lines were drawn. The old, old lines—even now, when so many of us are old, and you think we would have grown tired of it. The struggle on opposite ends of the tug-of-rope, the barnyard pecking order. I could smell it the minute I walked into the committee room. Fair enough— I, too, have done it all my life. Modern science requires its Metternichs no less than its Kochs.

But the girl, the child in quasi-military uniform, hadn't a clue. They were going to sacrifice her without a qualm, sending her unarmed and ignorant in front of charging cavalry. I did what I could to prevent it, until, with the passionate obstinacy of the young, she dashed out and flung herself in the path of the onrushing horses and was trampled.

When she'd gone, trembling and red-faced and defiant and pathetic, we got down to the real fight.

"I think," began Congressman John Leonard, committee chair, relatively young and politically ambitious. A Bible Belt Republican, his constituency believed passionately in shared responsibility, including the responsibility to regulate godless tampering with the human genome. They also believed passionately in family, including children, which meant a cure for the world's falling sperm count.

Congressman Leonard balanced delicately between these two beliefs. Regularly he assured the folks back home that the "sterile-intellectual forces subverting true humanity" were being well and manfully held in check by the United States government. He also regularly assured them that this same government was bravely exploring for a sterility cure. But despite this precarious fence-walking, Leonard's statement was true—he did think. Constantly, craftily, narrowly. He said, "I think we've established that Private Walders's testimony is not reliable."

"I agree," said Leah Janson, of the Pharmaceutical Manufacturers' Association, which spent billions yearly to convince the public that the gene-therapy drugs they manufactured had no connection whatsoever—*none*, not in a million years—with any technique that could be used to create any "inhuman monsters." "This girl has a history of lying and attention-grabbing."

"I think we're all in substantial agreement here," said Satish Gupta, National Institutes of Health, an honorable man deeply interested in the sperm-count crisis. His work, which focused on reversing poor sperm motility through manipulating *in utero* conditions, was one of the few lights of hope in the current darkness. I'd worked with him at the Nielson Institute. Gupta was rigidly truthful, with the genuine scientist's contempt for those who falsify data—even data about curfew violations.

"I'm not really so sure—" began Congressman Paul Letine, but he was a freshman, only thirty-two years old, from an unimportant state, and nobody listened.

I, however, am a personal appointee to this committee by the Vice President, courtesy of Vanderbilt Grant, one of the most powerful men in Washington. Grant headed the Food and Drug Administration, which had evolved great power since the Haxilent tragedy. Haxilent, a genetically engineered medicine remarkably effective against hypertension, had ended up killing 7,243 people through a freak, selective side effect. Now the FDA, according to its own PR, was all that stood between innocent Americans and a recurrence of that kind of recombinant roulette. To much of the public, Grant and his FDA army were a thin red line of heroes.

"I'm not really so sure—" freshman Letine said, and I broke in with, "I'm not so sure, either." The committee looked at me through that opaque distance that a challenge to power always creates. Eyes, turned to me respectfully, nonetheless narrowed.

"Private Walders may or may not be telling the truth," I said diplomatically, although I believed she was. That kind of stupid, youthful, self-destructive passion almost always meant truth. Liars are more self-protective; sociopaths less stupid. "But there's a strong chance that she saw exactly what she said she saw. Created not through germ-line manipulation, but through vivifacture."

No one looked surprised; they'd all expected this. Vivifacture was what I once did, why I'm now a member of this committee. Vivifacture, the engineering of human tissue, was the back door into changing a living body. Not inheritable, and so not illegal. Not contagious, and so not illegal. But not exactly religious or responsible, either.

Vivifacture doesn't alter DNA. But neither does it require pharmaceutical gene therapy, so drug companies aren't crazy about it. It competes for funding with basic research like Gupta's. And to many people, it's creepy. The public wanted replacement knees and fingers and tracheae and other cartilage-based parts—oh, how they wanted them! Not to mention how badly the rich desired replacement skin for aging faces and necks and upper arms. But they didn't like to think about how and where those parts were grown.

Over a biodegradable polymer "scaffold" on the soft underbelly of a dog bred without an immune system, nourished by the animal's blood nutrients. Under the skin of a rat. On the back of a lamb held motionless in restraints its whole immuno-compromised life.

Thus, despite its widespread medical and cosmetic uses, vivifacture wasn't discussed too openly in any official proceeding. After all, such meetings were recorded. Not too openly discussed, not too openly acted on, not too openly set out in the political arena against the lions of public opinion. This was one social responsibility that didn't get shared.

The wall screen still held the computer drawing of Private Walders's chimps, three hairy bodies with the same adorable human-child face. Glossy black child-hair, blond curls, spiky red hair with light freckles.

"Dr. Clementi, much as we appreciate your scientific contribution to this situation, it's paramount that we keep in mind the—"

"—possibilities that could have created this situation, yes," I said, smiling, unstoppable. They all knew I was here because Vanderbilt Grant put me here. "Let me just develop those possibilities a little. Vivifacture, as you all know, doesn't involve sperm or eggs. It doesn't involve the host's DNA at all. Rather, the needed organ—a human ear, a knee joint, a liver—is grown from samples of the recipient's own damaged organ, on or in a lab animal bred without—"

Chairman Leonard interrupted. "I'm sure we're all familiar with this level of explanation, Doctor. The medical advantages of vivifacture are well known."

They should be. This committee has had me force the details on them often enough. Although lately they might even welcome such vivifacture details, in preference to what else I've taken to forcing on them.

Leonard continued, "But as you yourself have testified for this committee, a brain—a whole *head*—is simply not possible to vivifacture. Computer software couldn't even design such a complex thing, let alone specify the needed scaffolding to grow it . . . that's what you've *told* us."

"And it's still true," I said.

"Then what Ms. Walders claimed to have noticed is impossible!" The chairman suddenly noticed that the drawing was still displayed on the wall screen. He said irritably, "Terminal off." The image disappeared.

I said, "It would be impossible if those chimps really did have human heads on simian bodies. But it would not be impossible if what they have is merely human faces, transplanted on top of their own, with the monkey skull surgically altered to human contours. Then they would merely *look* human. The brain, vocal cords, olfactory and hearing organs—all still simian. Only the optical nerves would need rewiring, and that's a common operation."

The freshman, Paul Letine, burst out, "And the hands?" I didn't even have to answer him. The entire world had been following the newsvid stories about Rashid Brown, third baseman for the Dallas Dodgers, who had lost his hand in a stupid accident and had it replaced with a new one of vivifactured skin over motor-powered plastic bones.

Susan O'Connor, CDC Genetic Integrity Task Force, frowned. "Let me be sure I understand this, Doctor. The chimps are—could be—real chimps, but covered with viv-ifactured human skin to resemble human children, but not on their bodies, which still look like monkeys—"

"—at least until they're dressed in little overalls and shoes," I said. I could see where she wanted to go.

"—and all this vivifacture, with its complex medical steps and need for bio-sealed areas for non-immune animals—all this was done in a *warehouse?* By unknown people, presumably scientists, without even a dossier on file with the FBI? I checked, Doctor—there is no dossier. So this secret, highly technical operation was carried out just a dozen miles from the Hill, from the Justice Department, at great expense, with superbly trained personnel . . . I'm sorry. I can't accept that premise. It just doesn't seem plausible."

"And *why* would anybody do it?" asked Letine.

Ah, freshmen. They never know what questions should not be asked because no one wants the answer in the record. I smiled at him.

"You're new to this committee, Congressman. Preliminary reports from the Nielson Institute were distributed over two years ago to everyone here, with speculative scenarios in the discipline of vivifacture. One such speculation concerned various ways to create pets that would lend themselves to even more anthropomorphism than the usual pet owner already indulges in."

He still didn't see it. "But *why?*"

I was getting tired. Rosaria, the attack by her mother, setting my fractured fingers . . . I tired much more easily these days. I expected it. Usually I could pace myself well enough that no one noticed, although it couldn't be long before Maggie did. Congressman Letine knew the answer to his own question, if he only thought about it.

The average artificial insemination was only effective for eighteen percent of couples seeking to have a child, and then only if they could afford the procedure in the first place. *In vitro* fertilization, which had a twenty-four percent success rate, cost even more. The average couple needed 2.6 tries at either to achieve pregnancy. The National Gene Pool Act limited a single sperm donor to successfully fertilizing a maximum of forty-two women; there were so few men left with viable sperm that any more inbreeding than that will have dire genetic consequences a few generations down the line. Equations proved this.

The result was that some people, of the millions who couldn't have children, would do anything to acquire a child. Anything.

Legally take one from the poor, through Child Protection.

Steal one.

Buy one, domestic or imported. Although Third-World children, for scientifically logical reasons no one would let me mention, were even scarcer than homegrown.

Or, if the prospective parents couldn't or wouldn't do any of that, they turned their pets into child substitutes. All over the country dogs ate in high chairs, cats inherited entire estates. A woman in Los Angeles, sad and lonely soul, killed herself when her pet rabbit died.

I said wearily to Letinc, "There would be a huge market for chimps that looked like babies. Among people who can't have children, and are desperate for what substitute they can get." With a light tan skin and hazel eyes and androgynous features that could be anything—Caucasian, Black, Hispanic, Asian, male or female—through just a little variation in hair and freckles. And you wouldn't even have to come up with college costs.

Letine sat very still. Then he mottled maroon, and dropped his eyes to hide their expression. So he and his wife were among the infertile; no surprise. And one of them—judging from his face, it was her—lavished parental frustration on something, although not a pet (what?). I felt sorry for him, which of course he would have hated.

Leah Janson said primly, to have it on the record, "Of course, there are laws against putting human parts into lesser species."

The record might as well be complete. I said, "The black market doesn't often regard the law."

"I really think," Chairman Leonard said, "that we've wandered pretty far from the point. All this is interesting, Dr. Clementi, and if you say it's theoretically possible, then of course we accept that. But the concern of this committee is to find out what is actually occurring—not theory, but fact. And there are no facts to back up Shana Walders's assertions. No trace left of the building she allegedly saw the man come out of. No trace of the man, or of the alleged animal experiments. And no reason to assume that Ms. Walders has been any more credible this time than during previous incidents in her official Service record."

"I agree," said Leah Janson.

"And I," said Satish Gupta, and Susan O'Connor, and everyone else around the table except James Letine, freshman, who said nothing.

"Then I think our report can conclude that this unsubstantiated, probably fabricated report does not merit additional follow-through," Leonard said. "Let the record show this as a unanimous committee decision."

Swept under the rug. And once more the Committee had avoided even touching on the larger problem. There was no more I could do, unless I wanted to file an official protest with Congress. That would involve conferences, media, power struggles, lawyers, turf wars. In the end, would anyone except the doctors and scientists believe me? And did it really matter if there were child-looking chimpanzees being put to bed in cribs and carried in Snuglis by desperate couples who would never have their own child? I had fathered three children. What right did I have to fight against the consolations of those born too late to have any?

And I just did not have the strength.

We cannot yet vivifacture a complex organ like a liver, let alone a brain. Not with our present level of knowledge and technology. Not even a lobe of the brain; it is simply too complex. We can shut down selective tissues in the brain, as is done to starve a tumor, or to induce such conditions as retrograde amnesia. We can wall off, cut out, or burn down other diseased areas. But none of that was going to help me. By the time it was detected, the mucormycosis fungus had already grown through both my nasal passages and the fragile skull bones behind, outstripping my aged immune system's ability to contain it. Long, slender, untouchable filaments of it penetrated the brain. I had, my doctors told me, perhaps another three months of mostly normal functioning, and then a few more months of dying.

I wanted to do it well.

Who, nowadays, cares for a well-crafted death? wrote Rainer Maria Rilke over a century ago. *Nobody. . . . it is rare to find anyone who wishes to have a death of his own. Long ago one carried death within oneself the way the fruit carries the pit within itself. The children had a small one inside and the adults a big one. The women carried it in their wombs and the men in their chests. One possessed it and there was a peculiar dignity and a quiet pride in that possession. . . .*

My fruit pit, carried in the right side of the brain, caused headaches, nasal infections, and periodic drooping of my right eye, especially when I was tired. I was tired now. I needed to go home, lie on the bed with Maggie in my arms, and tell her that I was fatally sick. That I wanted, above all, a well-crafted death, with dignity and pride. That I wanted to die quietly, wrapped in her tart and unfailing love, in our cabin in the Blue Ridge Mountains. With the woods behind me and the mountain below and the sky above, to await the distant but inevitable day when the death of the sun returned my atoms to the stars in which they were forged. I am neither a melodramatic nor a religious man, but this thought nonetheless comforted me; it was part of the thoughts I was collecting into myself for my serene death, even as I prepared to give up everything else I have loved. What I didn't want was to die in the midst of a media blitz about vivifacture, evil science, political incompetence, social responsibility, funding wars, religious hysteria, and politicians' rating polls.

The committee was watching me. Chairman Leonard said, "Dr. Clementi? Do you have anything to add?"

"No," I said. "Nothing to add."

Everyone smiled, and the committee meeting prepared to move on, and Shana Walders's future fell silently to guns she had never even had a chance to understand.

6

CAMERON ATULI

A week after Rob and I become lovers, I go outside the wall of Aldani House for the first time. Rob insists. Just a short walk, he says, how do you know you won't like it unless you try it?

I do like it. The first two blocks outside the gate are lined with pleasant houses, each with a small green lawn and a riot of flowers. The larger cross-street bustles with people enjoying the spring weather. A sturdy metal railing runs down the center of the sidewalk for anyone who might need it. There are outdoor cafes, music, marvelous little shops.

Essential Ingredients, with food from all over the world and a bakery window full of napoleons, marzipan, and madeleines.

Seasoned Beauties, a hair salon with "hairdressing, wigs, and transplants for the mature woman."

Searchlight, a public deebee search firm.

The Olde Toy Shoppe, its window full of dolls elaborately dressed in period costumes of antique cloth—are the dolls supposed to be for kids? They don't look like it, except for the inexpensive "Grandma Ann" dolls in one corner.

Tree House, a florist. The window displays gorgeous gen-emod flowers: purple-and-red striped roses, cluster lillies, and marilacs, the sweet-smelling lilacs that last two full weeks after you cut them.

A pharmacy, a law office, a home-security systems store, a clothing store specializing in "large and hard-to-fit sizes." A cafe, with well-dressed older people laughing and talking in the warm sunshine.

The jewelry store Rob mentioned, Jewel of the Ages, glitters and sparkles. I study the display.

"You're amazing," Rob says, a little hesitantly. "Watching you . . . I can't figure out if you recognize all this or if you're so fascinated because it seems new to you."

"Both," I say. It's true. As soon as I see each shop, I know what it's for, what the displays will be like. And yet I have no personal memory of them. Until I see a doll dressed like Marie Antoinette I can't imagine such a thing in the world, but as soon as I do see it, I both remember who Marie Antoinette is *and* know it for the first time. It's a giddy feeling, and suddenly I laugh.

"Let's buy that bracelet you told me about!"

We go inside and buy jewelry, but not for me. I find a bracelet of delicate lapis lazuli beads the exact color of Rob's eyes and insist on getting it for him. I slide my card into the display slot and the plastic opens itself. "Thank you for shopping with us!" the store says brightly. I clasp the bracelet on Rob's wrist, and he smiles at me before sliding it up under his sleeve, where no one else can see it.

On the street again, I'm careful not to hold Rob's hand. Nobody is blithe anymore in America, where everyone shares responsibility to keep society stable and cohesive and reproducing as much as possible. I remember this without trouble; it is a fact.

But people stare at us anyway, turning around in the

street. Because they can tell we're blithe? No, can't be; they're smiling. And it can't be because I'm Cameron Atuli—that's the whole point of modern ballet dancing in masks. The dance is what matters, not the dancer. Faces only distract from the form, the line, the movement.

Then a worse thought strikes me: Do these people rec ognize me from whatever happened before? Was my face, once, all over the newsvids and flimsies? *Does everyone glancing at me in the street know my life, when I don't?*

I ask Rob. "No, no," he says. "Oh, poor Cam, did you think that? No, it never hit the media. The police just talked to Melita and Mr. C., and they told the rest of us . . . some of it. But, no, nobody recognizes you from any of that."

"They're looking at me!"

"Of course they are," Rob says. "They're looking at both of us. Remember how few of us youngsters there are now."

And then I do remember. That, too, is a fact. The Tip- ping Point, the population shift . . . I never really cared much about any of it, and I still don't. The Tipping Point must have held no personal autobiographical meaning for me.

Most of the people going in and out of the shops look well-dressed and cheerful. This is a restricted area, Rob tells me, glow-marked for pre-approved entry. The people are mostly old, at least fifty, and Rob and I are young, and beautiful, and he moves like water. And so do I.

We shop some more, and eat Mexican food, and visit a VR parlor. Today's sim is Merry Old England, with bear baiting and troubadours and holo bawdiness and real ale. We start back late for rehearsal, and I don't even care.

At Linden Lane a woman comes around the corner

pushing a stroller. In the stroller is a puppy wearing a bonnet to protect its head from the sun. Carefully, so as not to jar the puppy, the woman lowers the stroller wheels over the curb.

"Cam!" Rob shouts. "Cam—what is it?"

But I'm already running, pushing other people off the sidewalk or into the center railing, staying as close to the building walls as I can for protection. Tears stream down my face, dried instantly by my speed. I run and run, Rob chasing me, and a part of my brain knows it's only Rob chasing me, not the dog in the sunbonnet—*just a puppy, just a puppy*—but I can't stop. When finally I have to, breathless, and Rob pants up to me, he can't touch me in public. But he makes me sit down, and brings me a soda, and all the time I'm seeing the puppy in the stroller and the woman's face above it, loving and doting as she fusses to get the stroller wheels over the curb, so careful not to jar her pathetic child substitute. And I can't stop shaking.

"Cameron," Rob says gently, not touching me, "tell me. Talk to me."

But I can't. There is nothing to tell. My memory is blank.

The next day I call Dr. Newell, and she comes to Aldani House and takes many readings on a portable medical machine. She inserts another patch, with slow-release pharmaceuticals, under my skin. Every day for a week she comes, personally, to Aldani House to check my readings. After a week she makes Rob and me go for another walk outside the walls.

I see another dog—on a leash this time, not in a stroller—and I feel my muscles tense for a moment, but that's all. I don't freak. Rob smiles at me warmly, and the rest of the walk is easy, even fun, although not as much fun as the first one.

And the dreams persist.

The company tour shatters everything.

We open with a gala in Washington, at the International Center. Four nights there. Then will come a private performance at the White House, but I'm not part of that, Sarah and Dmitri are principal dancers. But I'll go to New York, Montreal, London, Paris, Atlanta. The repertoire is the usual weird tour-mix: dances from some old chestnuts like *Prodigal Son* and *Synergy*, a few popular favorites like *String Theory*, some really interesting new work from people like Dana Stauffer and Elisabeth Beaudré, and even, Lord help us, the moldy old Black Swan *pas de deux* from *Swan Lake*. I dance six major roles and two supporting ones. Rob has three supporting roles, plus dancing in the corps de ballet. He needs to work on his extension.

The first night two blithe-bashers attack Rob and me on our way to the International Center. Or maybe they aren't blithe-bashers; maybe they just want money or drugs. Except that Rob doesn't believe that, and he's the one who knows Washington. I don't.

I don't know anything.

Not why we are attacked. Not why the blithe-bashers break off their attack and suddenly start to fight each other. And not how a soldier gets into my dressing room on the fourth night of the gala. No one can tell me that, not even after it's all over.

The International Center is only twenty years old, built just before the Tipping Point. Like all those buildings, it has formidable security. My dressing room is at the end of

a long corridor, all of it robocammed. At home of course
we don't have our own dressing rooms, but the International Center is huge, built to showcase Chinese circuses
and French opera and God knows what else, and we're
spread out. Rob and I aren't even sharing: too dangerous,
outside Aldani House. Although this hasn't slowed down
our sex, which is lovely.

I am dancing Horethal in *Dove Upon the Waters*, which is
typical for our repertoire away from Aldani House. Bibli-
cal ballets are big. The audience, Rob says, is full of politicians who believe God created man in his immutable
image, period—or at least pretend to believe that. Since
Horethal is destroyed at the end of the first act, when the
ark is already built and the rain starts, I go back to my
dressing room, warm and sweaty and magnificent in my
costume of vile decadence. This is part fabric, part body
paint, part tiny glued-on mirrors, and part holo, which creates snakes of light writhing constantly around my arms
and hips, between my legs, down my legs. Yum. Too bad
Rob doesn't get to wear the same thing. He's Shem, and
saved by God, and so dressed in a boring white tunic and
tights.

The corridor is empty. I close the door to my dressing
room, take off my mask, and switch off the holo—nobody needs snakes crawling over them offstage. I move to
my dressing table, and in the mirror I see the soldier, standing where the door was before I closed it. She moves toward me.

Immediately I scream. She levels her stun gun and says,
"You don't do that again. You really don't. Now, tell me
why I saw your face on three chimpanzees in the Lanham
train wreck."

I look wildly at the overhead robocam. It's dark. She must have disabled it, but doesn't that mean someone from Security will notice and come soon? Someone must come soon. The only thing I have to do is not let her hurt me until someone comes.

"On! Talk!" she says.

"I'm Horethal." They're the only words I can think of. "I'm Horethal."

"You're *what?*"

It's all that she gets time to say. The door flies open, Security crashes through, and the soldier goes down.

7

SHANA WALDERS

My National Service finishes up in July. The week before, my rejection from the Army comes in the mail.

On late Saturday afternoon I stand in my barracks and open the envelope—no email for this, the envelope is registered and certified. I slide out the letter. A single sentence, that's all the bastards give me:

6 July, 2034

Dear Shana Irene Walders:

The United States Army regrets to inform you that your application for induction has been refused, on the basis of your official National Service record, a copy of which is enclosed.

Sincerely,

Gen. Todd McHugh

(s) General Todd Winters McHugh
Recruitment, United States Army

The barracks is empty except for Meg Delany, snoring in her bunk. Everybody took the free afternoon and evening to go off-base. I waited for the mail. My skin goes hot, then cold. For a minute everything hurts.

Fuck 'em. Fuck 'em all.

I'll sue. My record don't look that bad! It was the Congressional hearing—they're deleting me because of what I said there. Because I told the truth.

Well, we'll see who can delete who! I'm a *youngster*, after all. A goddamn precious natural resource. There are agencies set up just to be sure us youngsters get whatever we need, if parents can't or won't get it for us—facilitation agencies, legal agencies. The Army can't do this to me. I'll sue. I'll go to the newsvids. They'll be damn sorry they tried to delete Shana Walders!

"What's that?" Meg Delany says sleepily, coming up behind me. I fold the letter in half and snarl at her. "Nothing!"

"If it's nothing, why do you look like you just got dropped from orbit?"

"Mind your own business, Delany."

"Ain't we touchy today!"

"Fuck off."

"Delete you."

Well, I will. I'll delete all of them, every single person that thinks they can stop Shana Walders from getting what she deserves.

Every single one.

I start with Legal Aid. It's a crummy storefront-type office on the edge of downtown D.C. The neighborhood is covered with government graffiti in superbright holos and real-people graffiti in spray paint. One covers the whole side of a foamcast building:

The Legal Aid office has a single not-too-clean window with electronic bars that flicker and shimmer, trying to make the dump look safe without looking like it's a jail. The furniture is the cheapest kind of lightweight foamcast, the kind that don't keep lice. The lawyer, a jellybelly older than rocks, reads my letter, studies my official record, and said, "Hmmmmm." Then silence.

" 'Hmmmmmm'?" I say. "That's it? You're an attorney here to help me and all you can say is 'hmmmm'?"

He looks at me over the top of the letter, that look official types all know how to give: *Who are you to question me and my vast experience, kid?* But I know who I am. I'm one kid who's going to get into the United States Army. Or else make them sorry as hell that they kept me out.

"Private Walders," he says, handing me back the letter, "in my opinion, you don't really have a case. Yes, your official record is borderline in terms of recruitment law—the Army could accept or reject someone with a record like yours. They've chosen to reject. A different recruitment committee might have ruled differently. But there is no legal precedent for challenging a local recruitment decision in circumstances like yours."

"So we'll be the first!"

"I don't think so. There's no real point."

"I'm the point!" I say, probably too loud. "This is my *life* we're talking about! The life of an American youngster!"

He gazes at me calmly. Finally he opens a drawer, takes out a card, and hands it to me. "I would advise you to plan a different life. This is net code for the Youth Career Facilitation Agency. Access them for an appointment for career testing."

"I don't need no career testing! I'm going to be a soldier!"

"I don't think so," he says.

"Then fuck what you think! I'll get a private lawyer who knows what he's doing!"

"You are free to do so, of course."

"I don't need you to tell me what I am or amn't free to do!" I stand up so fast my chair tips over. I don't pick it up. As I'm yanking open the door he talks to my back.

"Private Walders, an unsolicited piece of advice. Try to remember that not even a youngster is entitled to what she wants just because she wants it."

I don't answer, except to slam the door behind me.

I try two private lawyers. One won't even see me, after his system checks my credit-balance number. The other one tells me the same thing as the government jellybelly, but in even longer words.

I call up the *New York Times*.

The system eventually routes me to a live human being,

a bored-looking woman with sleek copper hair. Why do women that old use that color dye? She looks like a prune wearing a metal helmet.

"Yes?" Copper Head says. The screen is small, but I can see that she's seated in a cluttered cubicle somewhere— maybe New York, maybe telecommuting.

"My name is Shana Walders. And I've got a sensational story for you, ma'am. About a crooked Congressional committee."

"Your ID number, Ms. Walders?"

I give it to her. She gazes off to the left, and I know she's checking my public file. That's all right. I'm not illegal, not AWOL, not wanted for arrest, not on parole for sex crimes.

The image says, "And how do you happen to know anything about a Congressional committee? Please be advised that this conversation is being recorded."

I tell her the story. While I'm talking, she don't interrupt. But her face don't change expression, neither. When I'm done, she says, "An interesting story. The *Times* will follow through. If we need to contact you again, we will."

"That's it? You aren't going to . . . to ask me questions? Or start a big investigation?"

"The *Times* will follow through. If we need to contact you again, we will." The screen blanks.

I can't believe it. Here I hand her a terrific story—she could end up with a Nobel Prize or whatever they hand out to newspapers—and she just deletes me! What's wrong with the bitch?

But then I tell myself to calm down, maybe that's just standard newspaper procedure. After all, there are probably a lot of stewdees accessing them with really dumb leads. Venusians on their roofs, anti-grav inventions in their basements. Or people who aren't insane but who think every little thing in their lives belongs on the front page of the *Times*. I just need to wait patiently while she checks out my facts.

I wait a week.

Nothing happens, except that my Service officially ends. There's a ceremony, and a certificate, and my barracks sergeant says, "You have three days, Walders, to clear out of here. No more." Unlike my company sarge, she never liked me, the jealous cow.

After a week without hearing from the *Times*, and with nothing appearing on-line or in print about the Committee, I call up the *Washington Post-Tribune*. Then the Canby Vid Channel. Then two other vid channels. And nobody cares.

They care about more famine in India because there aren't enough farm workers left—that's page one of the *Times*. They care about the war in China, fought mostly by machines so's not to risk the young people—page one of the *Post*. About another fucking baby-stealing ring in Wichita lead story on Canby. About the riots in London, the military clampdown in Israel, the epidemic in Africa— but *not* about an American kid who's getting fucked by the system she only tried to serve by telling the truth.

My last night in the barracks, I'm so mad my brain burns. Nobody else is around. The company—the lucky ones still in Service—are out on an overnight park patrol. I'm supposed to be packing my stuff, but I keep stopping and just holding things in my hand, shirts and socks and music chips, for minutes at a time. Where am I supposed to go? I haven't got no parents waiting for me out there, no college acceptance, no job. I was supposed to be transferring to the army. Where the fuck am I supposed to go?

Somebody comes up behind me.

"Hey, Walders. Jumpy, ain't we?"

It's Bonnie DuFort, from C Company. She must of got left off park patrol again for bad conduct. She's the kind the army should be rejecting, not me.

"Fuck off, DuFort."

"I'm about to. Want to come?"

I look at her, not saying nothing.

"Yeah, I'm sitting in the corner with my widdle dunce cap again. And you're not even really here anymore. Why haven't you deleted this dump? Anyway, I'm not spending Saturday night around *here*. I'm going AWOL and meeting some she-wolves outside base and we're training into town to right us some shared-responsibility sins. Want to come?"

I shake my head no. I've never been one for rucky-fucky hunting—let the poor perverts do their sick thing, if they want to, who cares? DuFort don't, she's about as socially responsible as a cockroach. She don't want to right any sins, she just wants a fight.

"Still Little Miss Good Soldier," DuFort taunts. "Still playing by the system rules."

"Shut up, DuFort."

"Still thinks the system's going to reward her, just because she's a young-young-young-ster."

I throw the shirt I've been holding all this time—Service green, with the NS logo on the pocket—on the floor. "All right! I'm coming."

"Great," she says, and her eyes glitter.

We catch a train to D.C. and meet two of DuFort's friends in a bar. Teela and Dreamie. They're a little older, mid-twenties maybe, neither one pretty. Dreamie's reconfigured

on something, probably thunder, her hands twitching and
her eyes never still. Teela talks like she's short a few lobes.
Maybe burned 'em out. This isn't supposed to happen
to kids anymore—"tragic waste of our most precious
resource"—yeah, right. I'm up for whatever they're
planning.

Or at least, until I see what it is.

"Go down, us, to International. The rucky-fuckies there,
go in and out." Dreamie talks like that. I can't tell where
she's from. Maybe no place.

"On," DuFort agrees. "Go."

We catch another train. There's a second when the maglev kicks in and I flash on the derailment at Lanham, but
nothing happens to this train. We swing off in the high
city, tall buildings all around and the place swarming with
uniformed NSs working with the local cops. Traffic-and-
crowd-control details. My eyes prickle.

"Come on, Walders!" DuFort says. "Keep up!"

We go down a series of alleys between and over buildings, badly lit. Dreamie and Teela really know the terrain.
Finally we come out on a shallow ledge seven feet above the
ground and deep in shadow; the lights are below us,
shielded from weather by a little overhang. Beneath is a
small street leading to a locked door.

"Short cut for rucky-fucky actors," Dreamie's voice says
softly to my left. "Go down, those, to the thee-ay-tah. La
la la, rucky-fuckies."

I don't answer. We wait. Eventually two girls come out
of a nearby building and hurry toward the alley door. They
palm it and go inside.

"No," Dreamie says beside my ear, so soft it could be a
breeze stirring my hair. "Not girls. Not rucky-fucky."

We wait some more. As my eyes get used to the dark, I figure out that the smaller building opposite is a barracks or dorm or something, and the one right below us is part of the International Center. We're not that far from the Hill—or from the building where the Congressional committee fucked me over.

"La, la," Dreamie breathes. The door opposite opens again. Two men stroll across, close together. They're not holding hands, but it's clear from their silhouettes that they're together. Dreamie waits until they're directly underneath, then jumps.

She lands on one, takes him down. The other looks up—he can't help it, poor bastard, it's involuntary—and cries out. I see his upturned face clearly in the light above him, below us. Then Teela jumps, her feet knocking him onto the pavement. DuFort follows, giving a low, weird cry like nothing I hope to hear again.

I don't even think about it. I jump, too, and roll, coming up right beside Teela. She glances at me, smiling, knife in her hand. There's just time for her face to change one minute's worth before I knock the knife away from her victim's crotch and deck her with a right cross. She goes down.

Dreamie's on top of the other one, with DuFort at his head holding his arms flat on the pavement. She slashes open his tunic and tights, cutting his prick a little, but not really. She waits a bit for that, savoring. She never even sees the kick I aim at her chin. Her head snaps back and she falls, quiet.

DuFort lets go of the guy's arms. She don't know what's going on, but she knows she don't like it. She grabs up Dreamie's knife and squares off at me.

"I got no fight with you, DuFort. None."

She don't believe me. She circles, looking for an opening. I'm not armed, but I don't need to be. You learn a lot during the nights at government schools after the only kids left are the ones nobody wants to adopt. More than you learn in NS training. We circle, and feint, and it takes me a few minutes to get the knife away from her.

By that time, the rucky-fucky boys are gone. They stagger to the door, palm it, slam it. I disarm DuFort, take the knife, and start off running. I don't know the terrain, but she don't know it neither. I run through streets until I'm sure she's not on my ass, ditch the knife, and catch a train back to base. There I finish packing my stuff, call a cab, and go to a cheap hotel where NS lovers shack up. The air conditioning's broke. I lie on the bed, sweating, thinking.

The rucky-fucky boys got away inside all right. Not hurt.

I saw the one's face, tipped up in the light after Dreamie landed on his buddy.

It was a beautiful face: skin a light brown, not white and not black and not Hispanic and not Asian, but sort of all of them. Firm molded mouth. Big hazel eyes, flecked with gold. Small round chin. A different face, half kid and half not. A face that could be anything, any age. I'm good at faces. I always have been. It was fifteen years older on that actor, but I still know the face.

It was the same one I seen on the three chimps being carried away from the Lanham wreck.

The next day I go down to the train station to find a public terminal. Just my luck, the station's turned into a circus, with the government holding one of its stewdee Shared Responsibility Fairs. There's tables where volunteer doctors give patch vaccinations against whatever diseases feeble fusties get. There's booths for getting physicals from smart systems, and booths for getting vid information, and booths for kids to get their free Grandma Ann dolls and All Of Us! board games, booths for getting fucked over by this agency or that agency. The fusties going to these things are talking and laughing like its a big treat to trot around a dusty train station getting poked at by doctors and interviewed by charities. Poor bastards.

Music plays nonstop, real loud so anybody deaf can hear it. Stewdee stuff from the last century when these mossteeth were young. I try to close my ears to some fart bellowing about bridges and troubled waters. Wherever there isn't no booths, there's chairs jammed in so the geezers can sit down a lot, or railings so they can walk along without falling over.

To get to the public terminal, I have to squeeze between a blood-test table and a weird booth giving away pets to geezers. "Studies show that the care of a pet raises life expectancy, happiness, and personal-health index," the continuous-loop holo says, so cozy you want to barf on the whole program. Behind the holo is a live person, and behind him are stacked pens with kittens, puppies, and even rabbits. God, I hate rabbits. Twitching their nervous noses at you like they're afraid you'll squash them, scared of their own stewdee tails. But at least these rabbits looked healthy, not like the ones we saw more and more of in the woods behind the government school. Missing legs, stumpy ears. Once I saw one with three eyes.

On top of the loud music, there's yipping from the puppies and, of course, the noise of trains coming and going over on the maglevs. It's a fucking zoo.

"How much?" shouts a ragged moldy oldie at the blood-test table.

The nurse yells, "It's free if you're over seventy, ten dollars if you're not."

"And if you're over ninety they pay you," shouts another fusty, and everybody laughs.

I get to the terminal, put in my credit chip, and wait. First a whole long thing with flashy graphics comes up, urging young men to get tested for fertility ("It's a shared responsibility!") Finally the system actually gets around to asking me what I want, and I go brain-blank.

I know how to use a system, of course, but mostly I've just done the stuff everybody does: buy things, send mail, look up train schedules, snoop in files that their stewdee owners don't make secure. I know the public interacts can do a lot of other things, but I don't know what they are, and I don't know how to ask.

So I stare at the screen, which asks me again to proceed. Proceed how? I'm paying for these minutes. Finally I say, "I want to locate somebody, but I don't know his name."

"I'm sorry," the terminal says in that pleasant, stewdee voice they all have, "This system doesn't recognize your request. Please either phrase it in spoken computer, or use the typing option."

I don't know the spoken computer for this. You have to get the exact right words. So I type I want to find sumbody but I don't kno his name.

The terminal types back Enter current known information about subject person. Enter one item of information per line. It's stopped saying please. That makes me feel more comfortable. It's more like the Service.

I type:
He is a acter.
He is about twenty yeers old.
He has black hair.
He has hazle eyes.
He is about five feet ate inchs.
He ways about 150.
He is hansome.
He acts in Washington.
He is homosexal.

The computer types Public citizen information does not include physical appearance or police records. Do you wish a list of Stage Guild actors and/or Screen Guild actors and/or virtual reality Guild actors with Equity-registered appearances in Washington, D.C.?

Do I? Then I realize what an ass I'm being. I type He acts at the Internashunul Center. Right now. And there on the screen is the icon of a booklet.

I page through it. A lot of names, listed by the things they're in. There aren't just actors but also dancers, musicians. . . . I remember the glide-y way he and his rucky-fucky lover walked and I say aloud, "Print just the names of dancers."

The system don't know what I mean. So I page through the icon and print the list of every dance company in the summer season. There's five: a jazz, a holo/light troupe, an Asian thing, a black folk dance thing, and a ballet.

The amazing junk people will watch.

I shove the list in my pocket and push my way out of the station, through the feeble-fossil crowd and the horrible music and the rows of booths and the Project Patriot holosigns. UNITED WE STAND! and AMERICANS HELPING

AMERICANS! and YOUR FDA: PROTECTING YOU AND YOUR LOVED ONES. I go to find a cheap hotel. I don't have no choice. If I don't want to be noticed asking questions— and I don't—I'm going to be in D.C. a while. Fortunately, nobody can't spend much money confined to base, which I was a lot due to one thing or another, so I have credit saved up. It will last a few weeks. If I'm careful.

How much are tickets to the International Center? Maybe I can crash the gate. No, I can't. I can't do nothing to get me noticed before it's time. I'll have to actually pay good credit for the tickets.

Shit.

He's not in the jazz dances. Everybody on the playbill has danced by the end of the first act, so at least I get to leave. He's not in the holo/light troupe either, but at least the music don't fart and there's some good sfx. I fall asleep in the Asian folk dances, but that's all right because even though his looks could have been Asian—he could have been almost anything—these dancers are really from Asia and I don't think he's one of them.

The ballet dancers dance in masks.

In fucking *masks*. They're part of the costumes, part cloth or plastic or something and part holo, and they make the dancers look like birds or lights or fairies or whatever the hell they're supposed to be. But there's no way to identify anybody, and there are sixteen male names listed in the playbill.

I squint at the stage through my zooms. From here, all the men look the same: slender, muscular, graceful, not real tall. He could be any of them, or none of them.

I'm getting ready to storm out when I get an idea.

The playbill, which I studied while waiting for the dancing to start, is probably printed fresh every day. but it has a "Season's Substitutions" page, so you can see how often you didn't get to see the performers you paid to see. Stupid idea. But some clenched-asshole computer type wanted to make the record complete. And there it is, the night Dreamie and Teela hit the rucky-fuckies:

> ****Substituting for CAMERON ATULI in *Dances at a Gathering* and *Moscow Morning* pas de deux: MITCHELL REYNOLDS**
> ****Substituting for ROBERT RADISSON in *Moderate Environment:* ALONSO PERES**

Two dancers with bumps on their heads from being jumped on from seven feet up. One with a knife-nicked cock. But both back dancing the next night.

Cameron Atuli or Robert Radisson.

They both dance before intermission, some shit about a flood. Radisson, according to the playbill, is the stewdee standing around in a simple tunic, shifting his body every few minutes from one stupid pose to another. Atuli is a star. He dances in almost every scene, jumping and running and lifting some bitch who looks like she's flying, although it's probably all holo. I watch the whole damn ballet, until I'm sure. From his body movements when he lunges from her, the way he drops to his knees when they're done making love, the angle he throws back his head to fake a howl. I can't explain it, but I'm sure. The guy in the alley was Cameron Atuli, and it was Cameron Atuli's face on the chimps in Lanham.

The audience, all rusty fusties naturally, are going crazy: standing and clapping and yelling "Bravo!" I think the old lady next to me is going to have a heart attack, she's so excited. An old gas attack behind me keeps saying, "The tradition lives. No matter what, Cissy, the tradition lives," until I want to turn around and pop him. Tradition, my asshole. Good sperm is drying up and the country is moving into wheelchairs and youngsters like me are shattering ourselves trying to support all the old fucks, and this guy is thrilled out of his mind about the ballet tradition.

But I don't want to call no attention to myself, so I leave quiet, clutching the playbill that tells me when Cameron Atuli will dance next.

I've already decided it has to be the International Center. The building plans are on public terminal: "an architectural treasure." Any other building, a hotel or barracks or shit, and I'd be going in blind. Outdoors is too public, unless Atuli still uses the alley between his dorm and the Center. He probably don't. Nobody's that stupid.

I know how I'll get into the Center. You can't bribe electronic security systems, but you can bribe computer rustlers. I know some, from my days before the Service. They're expensive, and I don't have much money, but that's not the only way to pay. Most of the really good rustlers are old, they grew up when computers did, and I'm a gorgeous kid.

And it all goes right. The rustler gets me in, and I find Atuli's dressing room because his *name* is on the door program, and I wait. He strolls in, closes the door, switches off his holo costume of wiggling snakes. He takes off his mask. It's the same face. He looks in the mirror, smiling at himself, and he sees me. I move in front of the door.

He screams. I draw a stun gun—not the real thing, I can't afford the real thing, but this rucky-fucky don't know that—and say, "You don't do that again. You really don't. Now, tell me why I saw your face on three chimpanzees in the Lanham train wreck."

And it's like he don't even hear me. He's looking around the room like there must be another door, which there isn't. The old rustler I fucked shut down the security system for only ten minutes, with something called micro-intrusion, that he swore would confuse all the techie types while I got the info and got out.

I say, "On! Talk!"

And the rucky-fucky gabbles, "I'm Horethal. I'm Horethal."

"You're *what?*" But my old rustler didn't give me enough time, or he wasn't good enough, or he screwed me. Because all of a sudden the door flies down and somebody with a real stun gun crashes through. And I go down.

8

NICK CLEMENTI

Omar Khayyam was wrong.

The moving finger, having writ, *does* go back and wash out. It does so by making what was sweet then, seem sour now, because it has all turned out so badly. The finger smudges the memory, and so smudges the past, which is all and only memory.

My son had been a sweet child. There are vids of him at infancy, at two, at three—Maggie took a lot of vids of the children. Perhaps especially of John, the late-born child, the only boy, with his beautiful smile and wide brown eyes and fair skin flushed pink with health and activity. Maybe that was the problem. Sometimes beautiful people don't know they must eventually become more.

One warm July afternoon I returned from the labored daily walk I made myself take with the aid of a walking stick. The stick, an antique, was tipped with the carved head of an ass. This pleased me, but didn't make the walk any easier. Each day I walked less far.

John waited for me at the house, slouched in one of Maggie's cheerfully flowered chairs, sipping bourbon. Scowling. I braced myself, the small imperceptible raising of mental shields, in itself dismaying when it's your own child.

"Hello, John."

"Dad."

"I'm glad to see you. Where's your mother?"

"How should I know? I let myself in." He poured himself another bourbon from the sideboard. "Aren't you even going to ask why I'm here at this hour?"

It was 2:30 in the afternoon. "Certainly. Just let me get myself settled. . . . Can I get you anything?"

"I'm fine."

I put away my walking stick and poured myself a scotch. Maggie had filled the fireplace opening with a basket of roses and heliotrope, and the heavy scent floated on the warm air. I settled myself in the wing chair opposite John. He waited, moody.

"Now, then. What can I do for you, John?"

"You can't *do* anything for me," he said, ready to be irritated. "Every time I come and visit it isn't because I want you to *do* something for me."

"All right," I said evenly. "Then, how are you?"

"Smeared." John was thirty-six, but he used the slang of current adolescents. Perhaps this came from staying, in essence, the youngest generation. He and his wife, like so many others, were childless. John was among the eighty-plus percent of males whose sperm count was below five million per milliliter of semen: he was functionally sterile. A hundred years ago, young men of John's age averaged over a hundred million sperm per milliliter. His and Laurie's tries at *in vitro* had not taken.

"I'm sorry to hear that," I said. "Why are you 'smeared'?"

"I've been fired again."

He said this almost with sullen satisfaction: *see, the world is against me, I told you so.* I said, "How did that come about?"

"How should I know? I'm the fired one, not the firer. They just called this morning and said my telecommuting access was terminated." He sipped his bourbon.

He was still handsome. Or would be it it weren't for a certain puffiness, less physical than postural. His face sagged, his mouth sneered, his body slumped.

I said carefully, "What are you going to do?"

"What can I do? Look for another job. Laurie and I need the money."

He wouldn't have any trouble finding another job: there weren't enough workers to create everything needed by the huge population of old people. Poor old people supported—minimally—by taxes. Rich old people who hadn't yet passed on their money to their children, who therefore were doubly in need. That was what the last part of John's statement referred to. I ignored it.

"How is Laurie?"

"Fine." He actually smiled. John's wife was a treasure, a miracle, and sometimes the only way I could find to appreciate my son was that he had the good sense to appreciate Laurie. Maggie and I hoped desperately that she would never leave him.

I said, "Aren't you two supposed to come for dinner tomorrow night? Sallie and Richard will be up from Atlanta."

His smile vanished. "I don't know if I'll be up to a family party. You don't seem to realize, Dad, how tough it is to be laid off again. *You* never had to worry about that, of course."

Meaning, *you the successful scientist and over-achiever who haven't had the economic struggle I have.* There was enough truth in this whining implication to keep me quiet. My generation didn't carry a huge demographic bulge on our backs. On the other hand, being fired—which, I noticed, had now become "laid off" in John's mind—was a lot more common to my generation than his. I didn't say this.

I changed the subject. "Sallie will be sorry to miss you."

"I doubt it." John didn't like his older sister. Jealousy, perhaps. Sallie had always been a success: outstanding student, happy wife, respected senior researcher at the CDC. And never having wanted kids, she wasn't disappointed at not having them.

"Well, I better be going," John said gloomily. "I should be on the net, trying for some sort of job. Listen, tell Mom about the lay-off, will you? I just can't face another round of 'John-the-irresponsible.' "

Then become responsible, I wanted to say. *Complete your job duties, pay attention to your superiors, don't lie to cover up your mistakes.* It was usually the lying that did John in. Maggie, the most ethical person I've ever known, was driven wild by John's lying. I retreated from conflict with John. Maggie had never retreated in her life.

"I'll tell her," I said. "Think again about tomorrow night, John. Laurie always seems to enjoy coming here."

"Yeah." But no smile this time. "Of course, I know it's Laurie you want to see and not me."

"No, it's both of you," I said evenly. "Good luck with the job search."

"Sure."

He left, having never asked about my cane or unsteady walk or drooping right eye. I poured myself the second drink forbidden by my doctor but required by the situation.

Here is one of the hardest sentences for a parent to ever think: *I don't like my child.*

Be fair, Maggie's voice said in my head. *He and Laurie want a baby so much . . . the strain must be enormous.*

Yes, I could grant that. Although I suspected the strain was mostly on Laurie, not John. There are women in whom the desire to nourish and love a child is more than desire: it's a biological hunger. John, it sometimes seemed to me, was less interested in becoming a father than in feeling victimized because he wasn't. A year or so ago, he'd "accidentally" emailed me an entry from his diary files:

> *My father, Dr. Nicholas Clementi, claims descent from Muzio Clementi, the incredibly popular contemporary of Mozart. Clementi was the keyboard virtuoso of his day. He influenced Hayden and Beethoven and was buried in Westminster Abbey. Today Clementi is forgotten; Mozart is a legend. My father's claim is supposed to show that he is wryly modest about his own staggering professional reputation. Sic transit gloria mundi, even a gloria anchored by microbiology. It's as if he assumes that age must be accompanied by mystical, detached wisdom, and so if he has age, he must also have the other and is obliged to display it. And he does. My father is wise all over the place.*
>
> *I, on the other hand, never mention Muzio Clementi. If you're not going to have any descendants to carry on your name, why care who brought it to you?*

I wandered around the living room, touching Maggie's bibelots. A brass urn, a table sculpture, a candy bowl, a framed picture of our mountain cabin. I needed to distract myself. But I couldn't seem to concentrate on my scientific journals, or even on the TV, which gave me a program about "the so-called problem of endocrine disrupters leaching from household plastics." The problem, said a handsome actor in a white lab coat, was imaginary, supposedly derived from a few badly designed studies. The public should be reassured by the heroic watchdog activities of the FDA, by the even worse problems we would have without household plastics, and by the much-better-designed studies he would quote now. Both studies and program, I noted, had been made possible by "a generous grant from the American Plastics Foundation."

I was grateful when the house system interrupted. "Dr. Clementi, you have an incoming vidcall."

I took it on my wrister. A computer voice announced, "This call originates from Prince Georges County Correctional Facility," and then she came on, a tiny image looking disheveled and furious.

"Dr. Clementi? This is Shana Walders. I'm calling from *jail.*"

"Yes, Private Walders."

That acceptance seemed to disconcert her. "Well, they arrested me! And I think you got an obligation to help me!"

"And why is that? Because I'm the one responsible for your arrest?" More victimization. More John.

She scowled fiercely. "Well, no, I guess I did that."

I sat up straighter. "House, transfer this call back to your system, please." It did, and Shana Walders's face appeared, much larger, on my wall screen. Her golden hair was a tangled mess, and there was a bruise on her left cheek. Resisting arrest, I would guess.

She said, "I'm responsible for getting myself arrested, but *you're* responsible for me not getting into the army. That Congress hearing! So I think you should help me now." Pause. "Please."

"I don't see why I should—"

"They're only letting me have this one phone call!" she said, and started to cry. Suddenly she looked very young and very defenseless.

"Private Walders, I am not moved by tears," I said austerely, and instantly the tears vanished. She was versatile. "However, I can be reached by logic. Why don't you calmly explain to me just what has happened."

"All right. I found the boy whose face was on those stupid monkeys."

I hadn't expected to hear that. "And how did you accomplish this?"

She explained the entire brainless sequence, starting with the girls' attack on the young men. That sort of stupid bigotry in itself was enough to disgust me, but then much of the current political climate disgusted me. I listened quietly, through her search for the right dancer, her ill-planned trespass in the International Center, her arrest.

"Private Walders, did the authorities use a truth drug?"

"Of course. I said they could. I don't have nothing to hide here!"

Shana Walders's image glared at me ferociously. Clearly, they hadn't progressed to any of the other drugs used to control prisoners in a system so short of cash that often only two guards ran an entire prison shift. She was so ferocious, so vivid, so prepared to fight hard for whatever she thought she wanted.

So unlike John.

"All right," I said, "against my better judgment, I'll come down and bail you out. At least until I can check out your story."

"Thank you!" she said, and smiled up through suddenly lowered, suddenly dewy lashes. It was like the sun rising. Surely she wasn't stupid enough to try sexual wiles on me? Maggie would be amused.

"Don't slug anyone else until I get there," I said, and rose slowly to retrieve my walking stick.

"Where do you live?" I said to Shana, leaning on my stick outside the county jail, which was being used for the considerable overflow from D.C. itself. Bail had, of course, been nominal. The system needed to keep inside as few people as possible, and unless they had actually maimed someone, eighteen-year-olds were treated indulgently. They're a precious national resource, as the ad campaigns endlessly remind us. In actuality, the ubiquitous holosigns of Project Patriot exist not to remind us oldsters, who know full well how dependent we are on the young working force, but to remind the young of their obligations to us. Through flattery, through community, through anything that might work. YOUR COUNTRY NEEDS YOU!

"I don't live no place," Shana said. "I'm pretty much out of money." She looked at me expectantly, and moved closer.

"Private Walders, let us get have one thing perfectly understood between us. I'm old enough to be your grandfather. Possibly your great-grandfather. I'm also married, very happily. If I've interested myself in your story, it's because your story interests me, not your body."

She stared at me in complete disbelief. And then smiled, shaking her head. "Oh, sure, right."

What had this child's life been like? Never mind; I could guess. *Love at first sight is vague until/ Gold's tinkling makes him audible. . . .* Rosetti. But Shana *was* versatile. She moved away from me—I had the definite impression she considered this only temporary—and turned brisk. "Okay, what else can I tell you about my story? And can I tell it to you at your place, so I'm not out on the street? I'm too old for Child Protection."

They'd take her in anyway. Nobody refused to help a youngster. Including, apparently, me. "Yes, you may stay with my wife and me. That way I can make sure you don't jump bail."

She smiled at the thought that I could make her do anything, and followed my careful walk toward the train. "You need help?"

"No." And then, "Thank you."

She nodded, and slowed her pace to mine, and all of a sudden I was aware how sweet it was to have a youngster walking beside me, trustfully depending on me. This was how it had felt when Sallie and Alana and John were young. To a child, daddy was a superman. If Alana and her little family hadn't emigrated to Mars . . . if Sallie or John had given us grandchildren . . .

"Watch that curb," Shana said, and took my arm. I watched the older old people around me in mid-afternoon, people with no place in particular to go. A woman feeding pigeons. Two men playing backgammon on a safely monitored bench. On a low foamcast wall someone had spray-painted GEEZERS DIE AND LET US FREE! Nobody looked directly at the graffiti. Instead they shot me sideways glances, me with my beautiful granddaughter, one of the lucky few, why me and not them? I didn't meet their eyes.

Our progress was slow. My headache had returned, despite the massive dose of painkillers I'd prescribed myself along with the antifungal drugs. The drugs retarded the growth of the mucormycosis, but hadn't been able to eradicate it completely. Mucor was like that. Stubborn and persistent as Shana Walders. It was growing through the nerves connected to my brain.

"Look at that," Shana said, and pointed with the hand not holding me up. Across the street, a child of about eight had spotted a rat behind some garbage cans. The little boy approached it curiously. His bodyguard, a huge burly woman in uniform, grabbed the child's hand and led him away from the trash. Immediately the child threw himself to the ground and began screaming, fighting to break the woman's grip, kicking his heels on the dirty pavement. The rat, unalarmed, watched from behind a trash bin, baring its teeth.

Shana said, "If that kid was mine, I'd whack him so hard his head wouldn't stop ringing for a week. He's too old for that shit. Look at him!"

I could feel my right eye droop again. I said wearily, "Diminished tolerance for frustration. Or a learning disability. Or perhaps just considerably increased aggression, like the rat. All the result of increased hormone disrupters."

"What?"

"Nothing," I said. "You wouldn't believe it." Like everybody else.

"I'm not *stupid*," the girl said angrily. But I was too tired, too muffled in pain, to answer her. Too busy dying.

None of that. No self-pity. *Cowards die many times before their deaths; The valiant never taste of death but once.* Shakespeare.

We waited, Shana and I, for a cab.

Maggie eyed Shana warily. "Are you willing to give me your personal code to your citizen's file?"

"So you can look up my police record?"

"Exactly," Maggie said. They looked at each other, Shana in very short yellow shorts and garish one-shouldered sweater, her hair a golden tangle; Maggie in a simple, expensive dress the same soft white as her pretty curls. Separated by more than half a century, they wore identical expressions: smiling, hostile, determined. I moved out from between them and lowered myself to the sofa. When she'd first entered my living room, Shana had looked around with fake, hungry disdain, taking in the sculptures, the old-fashioned books, paintings, carved moldings, deeply lacquered walls. Maggie didn't like wall programming. Our house was traditional, serene, and in it Shana Walders looked like a misprojected pornographic holo.

She said, "And if I don't give you my personal code, I'm out on the street?"

"You are."

"Then I don't got much choice, do I?"

"Certainly you do. Give me the code or don't give me the code. Whine about each choice having consequences, or don't whine."

Shana flushed. She didn't like being accused of whining. "XDG609K327!"

"Thank you," Maggie said, and left the room.

Shana said grudgingly, "That's one tough old mare."

"Tougher than I am," I said, and the girl laughed. When she threw back her head, the strong white column of her throat shone. I saw why she expected slavishness from men. *Only God, my dear, / Could love you for yourself alone / And not your yellow hair.* If I were twenty years younger . . . no, not even then. She was a lethal gene just waiting for expression.

Maggie returned. "Juvenile records sealed, and in the last year she's been in Service. What's in the sealed juvies, dear?"

"Two burglaries, one assault."

"Details?"

"The assault was a bar fight on a girl who got too friendly with a man I was fucking. The burglaries were jewelry from houses pretty much like this one."

I was appalled. I hadn't expected all this. But Maggie only said, "I see. Juvenile house restraint?"

"Suspended sentences." Shana smiled. "I'm a precious natural resource."

"And an unethical shit," Maggie said cheerfully. "However, your retina scan is now on file. If anything turns up missing from this house, you'd be very easy to track. And you're no longer a juvenile. Adult sentences are no fun." Crime is rarer now—old people tend to behave—but sentences are heavier. Personal responsibility.

"How do you know," Shana said, "that I won't just murder you both in your beds?"

"Because you're not a damn fool," Maggie said. "Just remember, dear, that I'm not, either. Nick, what's wrong with your eye?"

"Nothing," I lied. I could see she didn't believe me, but she wouldn't make an issue of it in front of Shana. Soon I would have to tell Maggie about the mucormycosis. Soon.

"Then," she said, "I'll just see about dinner." And she left Shana and me alone to talk.

"Well, I'm glad *she* wasn't my sergeant," Shana said sullenly. "So what do we do now?"

I'd been thinking about that. Vivifacturing could, in theory, duplicate a living face and graft it over a bone-altered chimp's. But it would require polymer scaffolds of great complexity upon which to grow various kinds of cells from their originals. The scaffolds are computer-constructed from MOSSs—Multi-layer Organ-Structure Scans. To obtain a MOSS of that detail, the subject—or, in this case, his head and hands—must have spent hours inside a MOSS tank. Also, cell sampling would take a long while; you'd need to obtain several hundred different prototypes, from blood vessels to fat cells. And, of course, the use the prototypes had been put to was wildly illegal, even though it didn't actually tamper with human DNA. After that prohibition, the second genetic commandment was "Thou shalt not pollute the human form by crossing it with animals."

So young Cameron Atuli had to have cooperated in putting his face on chimpanzees.

But that didn't make sense either. Like Maggie, I'd left Shana alone in the living room long enough for hasty research in the deebees. Cameron Atuli was one of the world's most promising young dancers. I'm not much interested in ballet, but there are those who are, and they raved that Atuli was "luminous," "radiant," "penetrating," "dazzlingly fast"—all those wavelength-oriented adjectives so curiously applied to performance art. Atuli had a brilliant future. It would make him rich, if he wasn't already.

And he was insularly, discreetly homosexual, which meant he would do well to keep a low off-stage profile. He had no reason to be part of an illegal tissue engineering experiment, and much reason not to. It didn't make sense.

Unless either he'd been blackmailed into cooperation, or the MOSS and tissue samples had been taken without his consent. Blackmail was always a possibility for anyone gay—no, that was the word of my youth, it was "blithe" now—but for Atuli it didn't seem likely. The shared-responsibility crowd, religious or not, didn't go in much for ballet. The vids regarded it as an unimportant and dying cultural footnote. Atuli had, according to the records, no family to threaten (his parents, both soldiers, had died in South America) and no inherited fortune. And he lived in Aldani House. Endowed by a passionate patron, Aldani House was a safe, secluded oasis for dancers, of all sexual and political orientations. No, blackmail didn't seem likely.

"Hey, remember me?" Shana said. "I'm still here, Doctor!"

"Sorry," I said. "I was thinking. Our next step should be to talk to some people I know."

"What sort of people?"

"Police," I said, to see what she'd say. But Shana only nodded. I grew more and more sure that her story was true.

"Okay, police. Why?"

"Because there are things here that don't make sense."

"No kidding. Hey, something smells good."

"Dinner is served, Dr. Clementi," the house system said.

"About time. I'm fucking empty." Then she added casually, "You still eat okay?"

I led the way to the dining room. "What do you mean?"

"Don't try to woof *me*, Doctor. I been around old people my whole life. How much longer you got?"

I stopped cold and turned around to stare at her.

"Ooohhh," she said. "Your wife don't know yet."

"Shana—"

"On," she said. "I won't say nothing. What kind is it?"

She was so matter-of-fact. Were all the young like this, casually accepting death all around them? When I'd been young, death had been hidden away, in hospitals and nursing homes and back bedrooms. Now it wouldn't stay in those discreet cubbyholes; there was too much of it. Like weather, it was ubiquitous even when inconvenient.

Thou knowest 'tis common; all that live must die—

"I have a brain disease." It was an unexpected relief to say it aloud.

"Could be worse. You'll probably just pop off one of these days. What's for dinner, do you know?"

"Roast beef," I said, and had to laugh. *A well-crafted death*, I'd wanted. Among heirs for whom the craft was as common as breath. And as boring as ballet.

"Wonderful," Shana said. "I love roast beef. Let's eat."

The Commissioner of the Food and Drug Administration stood to greet me as I entered his office. "Nick!" he cried, taking both his hands in mine and smiling warmly, his eyes wary. I felt all over again, as I had felt for over fifty years, the intense contradictions in the man.

Vanderbilt Grant and I been at Harvard Medical School together, a million years ago in the 1970s. He had fascinated and bewildered me then—fascinated and bewildered all of us medical students from small, ordered towns with small, ordered lives. But Van's contradictions had begun long before Harvard. His father had been a black jazz musician; his mother a Vanderbilt, an American princess slumming in the New York "beat" scene in the 1950s; his birth a family scandal. Later, in the civil-rights era, ten-year-old Van had registered voters in a racially embattled South. At college, he'd been an angry black activist—but never a violent one. *Work within the system*, he'd urged students bent on storming the administration building, *and bring the fascists down that way.* "They gonna yield to what's *right.*" The ghetto slang was false; as radical grew chic, Van had taken to spending his summers with his Vanderbilt cousins at Newport and Bar Harbor. He was a wicked tennis player, and could have been an Olympic swimmer if he'd taken it seriously, which he didn't. "Nothing momentous was ever decided in a swimming pool."

Then he'd gone to medical school, graduating first in our class, and worked himself up to chief of medicine at New York Hospital in Queens. By 2020, he was married and rich, living on the water in Connecticut, dividing his spare time between golf and the free black clinics in the Bronx. His Wall Street friends respected his ability to invest his growing fortune cannily and well. His grandchildren attended Groton.

The Tipping Point changed all that. Blacks, disproportionate at the bottom of the social scale, were hit hard as government programs, even such basics as police, were slashed. Van left New York Hospital and took to the streets. He organized and preached—by this time he'd become a born-again Christian—and ordered and cajoled and, some say, personally kept much of New York from exploding into unstoppable destruction. When the crisis was over, he was a national figure. President Combes appointed him FDA Commissioner as the first act of his first term. Washington rumor was that Combes had personally begged Van Grant to take over the FDA. Somehow, Van was acceptable to everybody· religious, minorities, the scientific community, the poor, big business, even the drug companies. "You can reason with him," the pharmaceutical houses said, "he's not a rigid bureaucrat." Vanderbilt Grant was the first FDA Commissioner ever to attain an 82% public recognition rate. More Americans knew his name than knew who was Vice President.

His contradictions grew deeper than ever. Sincerely warm, and yet always with that reserve, that aloof place you could never touch. Genuinely compassionate toward the bottom level of society, and yet he advocated a stern morality of individual responsibility. Charismatic and self-righteous, ruthless and kind, black and conservative, Vanderbilt Grant forged his own way, smiling and bellowing, and the political pundits were always two steps behind. He changed position constantly, and never looked as if he waffled. Every position, he said, was deeply felt, and people believed it. He was the perfect Washington politician.

He was not a perfect friend, as I well knew. You couldn't get close enough to him. And yet it was Van Grant whom I'd asked to be best man at my wedding. Van Grant who had sponsored Alana as a candidate for Mars emigration. Van Grant who had plucked me, upon my retirement from the Institute, and basted me into the Congressional Advisory Committee for Medical Crises.

He stood in front of me now, holding both my hands, beaming. Wiry and upright, he looked fifteen years younger than I. His voice, that famous deep and melodious voice, was full of restrained power, like a good sax that might at any moment cut loose from the melody and really soar. It was a voice that people always remembered.

"It's good to see you again, Nick! How long has it been? Never mind, we don't need any reminders of our age." He laughed, a gut-deep chuckle, while his eyes studied me. I saw him note my drooping eye and bad color. Van had been a brilliant diagnostician. "What can I do for you, Nick?"

"A favor," I said, seating myself in a comfortable chair. Teak desk, leather chairs, the latest in wall programming, sculptures by black street artists, an American flag hand-embroidered. "I'm on the Congressional Advisory Committee for Medical Crises."

Van nodded; his recommendation had put me there.

"The Committee and I don't see eye-to-eye, Van, as you already know—but it's getting worse. They refuse to even *look* at the causes of the fertility crisis. Over and over I point out the studies—there are more of them every month—telling us that human infertility is caused by all the cumulative endocrine disrupters we've put into the environment."

Amazing studies, to anyone who read them. But most people preferred to look the other way. *Oh, it's mostly Africa,* they said, because that desperate continent had been the hardest hit, having used the most heavy chemicals in its futile attempts to control insects and crops and disease. But it wasn't mostly Africa. The majority of endocrine disrupters are wind-borne. The studies that the Congressional Advisory Committee so carefully ignored revealed critical accumulations of disrupters in the tissues of Arctic polar bears, of Pacific Island bush rats, of South American spider monkeys.

"The Committee keeps saying 'inconclusive evidence,' "
I continued, "because the data is evidential. Rather than
being the kind of thing you can subject to laboratory
proof."

Van nodded again; he knew all this, of course. Somehow he'd managed to support both sides at once, by publicly stressing that causes of a problem are less important
than solutions, and what can we do *now*? On him, it didn't
look like fence-sitting. It looked like a call to vigor and action.

I went on, "But my favor concerns something more specific than that. There's something besides butt-covering
and pig-headedness going on with the Committee. Listen to
this."

I retold Shana Walders's story, and the Committee's eagerness to dismiss it as lies. "Usually they jump on any
kind of animal-human hybrid and bray about it to the
media. It's a good way to get credit for action without actually doing anything, such as looking closely at endocrine
disrupters. But this time they want the possibility of an illegal hybrid to just go away. Why?"

Van steepled his fingers and considered, watching me
intently. He'd always been a good listener. "Well, Nick,
have you considered that more and more, Congress just
sort of stays away from *anything* involving vivifacture? That
could be the reason the Committee doesn't want to look
too deeply into your girl's story."

"I thought of that, of course. They don't want to get
the RPs all worked up over human knee joints grown on
baboons and cosmetic skin grafts grown on the backs of
cats. The less said, the better. But I think there's more going
on here."

"And why is that?"

I told him about Shana's tracking down Cameron Atuli. Van's face didn't change. When I'd finished, he said, "That's interesting. Fascinating, in fact. But I don't see what it's got to do with me. What are you asking for here?"

"I need an FBI case file search. To see if Cameron Atuli has been involved in any way with any illegal genetic or vivifacture activity. The Committee could request one officially, but I don't want it officially. I just want it."

"Can't do it, Nick. You know that. FDA and FBI are two separate organizations."

"Bullshit," I said genially. "Your investigators are out there in the field checking animal tests for new drug applications, monitoring clinical trials, polling outside experts for medical review. Your guys hear everything, including all the leads to illegal activity. You can't tell me, Van, that your organization hasn't gotten tighter and tighter with the FBI as the range of federal genetic violations has grown. You funnel information to the Bureau's Criminal Genetics Section all the time."

He was too smart to deny it. "And if we do? What makes you think it's a two-way street?"

"Because everything in Washington is," I said. "Van, don't treat me like—what do the kids say?—a 'stewdee.' A stupid deformity."

He gave me that sudden, blinding smile. "Never in this world, Nick. Not you. Okay, let's say I could theoretically find out if Cameron Atuli is on record as ever being involved in any illegal vivifacture. Why do you want to know?"

"I want to find out if Shana Walders's story really is true."

His voice, that amazing instrument, deepened a tone. "You've interested yourself in the girl."

"Well, the young are a natural resource, aren't they? So we keep saying. And she's a promising child."

Again that warm chuckle. And, casually, "How's John doing these days?"

"About the same." Oh, he was good. He'd let me know he understood why I might be driven to help a "promising" child. But he did it with the lightest touch.

"And Maggie? Seems ages since Helen and I saw you folks."

"She's fine. You'll help me on this, Van?"

"I will," he said, and laughed because it reminded both of us of the wedding ceremony, when I'd married Maggie with Van by my side. "You know I will."

"You'll find out if Cameron Atuli has any recorded involvement, as perpetrator or victim? With either genetic violations or vivifacture violations, up to and including kidnapping for cell samples?" With Van, it was best to make agreements clear and specific. He was too good at sliding out from under fuzzy ones.

"Yes."

"And can I count on hearing from you soon?"

His gaze strayed, seemingly casually, to my drooping eye, then back to my face. "This week, Nick."

"Thanks, Van."

I stood, aware of how shaky I must seem next to him, even though he was in fact a few years the elder. He would go on to a full afternoon's work; I wanted to go home and go to bed.

"Take care of yourself, Nick." In that rich voice, it was

a benediction. A prayer from the healthy, on behalf of the rest of us.

"Well?" Shana demanded, out on the street where I'd left her. An old man panhandled against the sunny south wall of the building. A woman walked past, pushing a stroller with two kittens in it. A holosign winked and revolved: WE CAN DO IT TOGETHER. SHARE THE COMMUNITY OF AMERICA! On the corner, a religious crazy teetered on the curb and shouted about the end of the world. His projector, very old, was malfunctioning: through the crude holos of tidal waves and earthquakes flickered scenes from what looked like an instructional holo on quilting. "Hey, Nick, you okay?"

Each of us earns our own death, which belongs to no one else. George Seferis.

"Yes," I said, "I'm doing fine. Let's go home."

9

CAMERON ATULI

It's an hour before the curtain goes up at Lincoln Center on *Jupiter Moon Suite,* and backstage is chaos. The guest dancers, Eric Carter of the Royal Ballet and Vivian Vargas of what is left of the New York City Ballet, are both pigs. Carter insulted Sarah, telling her that she moved like a tugboat, and Sarah ran out of rehearsal in tears. Vargas talks constantly about the past greatness of the NYCB, even though now it's a pathetic shambles. She makes it clear that she disdains Aldani House, but she is so beautiful that Dmitri follows her like a slave, greatly upsetting Laura, who is in love with him. Joaquim has torn a tendon and cannot dance the role of The Interloper. Tasha, for no reason anyone can see, snaps at everyone. The air prickles with tension.

I am hurrying along the dreary understage corridors to bring Joaquim more ice for his knee when Melita stops me. "Cameron, dear!"

"Yes?" This is bad. Melita, who is only in her fifties but dresses like a *grand dame,* is a superb business manager for Aldani House. Mr. C. couldn't manage without her. But no one would say she is warm. When she calls dancers "dear," we brace ourselves.

"It's about the reception after tonight's performance, dear. For the patrons."

I groan. NYCB, to whom Lincoln Center is still home, always needs money. Almost every performance, even by a visiting company, is followed by a "reception" to wring more money out of patrons by letting them mingle with dancers, most of whom hate it. It's very hard to talk to these corporate leaders and politicians and society ladies. They don't know very much about dance, and what they do know is wrong.

I say, "Raising money for the NYCB isn't our job. Let prima donna Vargas do it."

Melita ignores this, as she ignored my groan. Already dressed for the gala, she wears a diamond barrette in her hair. The barrette is fake, I know: the real one was sold long ago to finance a special production of *Mozartiana*. "Cameron, that's why I wanted to speak to you. Not all the fund raising tonight *will* be for NYCB. I've just heard that there's going to be present a patron ready to pledge Aldani House fifty thousand dollars. With that much, maybe we can mount a new ballet next season."

Her eyes shine; the Aldani House endowment covers the basics, but not such extravagances as a complete new ballet. I suddenly feel contrite. Melita is as committed to Aldani House as any of us dancers—maybe more. "All right, Melita, I'll come and mingle."

"You'll do more than that. This woman has asked specifically to meet you. She's a great admirer. I want you to talk to her, and her alone, for at least a half hour straight. No, don't look like that—she's very easy to talk to."

I'm appalled. Half an hour! "I can't!"

"Half an hour straight, Cameron. Her name is Mrs. Justine Locke. And dance well, dear." She waves her hand and bustles on down the corridor, her evening gown swishing, while I stand there with Joaquim's ice melting all over my hands.

The performance goes well enough, although Mitchell is not really up to Joaquim's role and the decaying New York State Theater is less than a third full. New York is a financial ruin, Rob told me; it's possible that NYCB will not survive at all. Also, Laura is clearly fighting back tears and stumbles on a simple *pas de chat*. But Eric Carter, damn his beautiful shoulders, dances Jupiter like the god himself, and the third movement of the suite, "Europa," has an energy and harmony that brings the small audience to its feet.

Afterwards, still in my sweaty costume, I go reluctantly to the Promenade. The Promenade is a great empty indoor plaza surrounded by walls of glass, which are noticeably dirty. Three tiers of wrought-iron balconies circle the glass, but they're too shaky to stand on. On the stairs, badly mended slashes in the red carpet look dangerous to high heels. I pass empty pedestals where, Vivian Vargas said, there once stood huge dramatic sculptures. She doesn't know of what. They were sold to pay Lincoln Center utilities before Vargas even joined the company. Now the lighting is dim everywhere except at the party itself, and even there it couldn't be called bright. Maybe patrons find that romantic.

But please God, not this particular patron. If Melita has set me up to have to fend off some amorous rich society woman . . .

But Justine Locke isn't amorous, and she isn't young. At least seventy, maybe more. She wears a lovely magenta gown, very simple, without holo-enhancements or jewels. Her eyes are sunken but her skin is smooth; vivifactured, probably. She introduces herself to me shyly. And she actually knows something about ballet.

"What was wrong with Tasha Riccio tonight?" she asks, after we've been chatting aimlessly a while. "I thought she was a bit off."

"She was."

"I'm watching her; she has promise, don't you think? And besides, she looks like my granddaughter."

She smiles suddenly, an abashed smile, as if it's silly to expect me to care that Tasha looks like her granddaughter. All of a sudden, I feel more at ease. So I say, "Do you have a picture of your granddaughter?"

"Oh, you don't want to see that."

"Sure, I do." Deference is rare among patrons; they're too aware that they control what Melita calls "the green river of life."

Mrs. Locke pulls out a packet of holograms from her evening purse, and that touches me, too, that she would carry them around even in her small gold bag. The older granddaughter does look like Tasha. And the other one, three years old, is enchanting.

"You like kids," Mrs. Locke says, her kindly old eyes smiling at me. "Do you have any brothers or sisters?"

You will wonder a thousand times what's in those memories. "No. No, I don't."

"Pity. I'm very fortunate, in these times, to have two grandchildren. So many of my friends have none. Although the younger one is . . . adopted. You may have noticed she doesn't look like her sister."

"No, she doesn't."

"She came to us by a . . . complicated route. Not strictly

conventional. But perhaps you disapprove of such an intense desire to have children that one . . . bends the rules."

"Well, no," I say. I've never thought about it. The kindly, sunken eyes are suddenly very sharp, watching me. She says nothing, which makes me feel I have to fill the silence. "I mean, yes. . . . I guess you shouldn't bend the rules about kids. The laws are there to protect them, right? The government probably knows what's it's doing with those laws." I feel like an idiot; this subject doesn't interest me, and so I don't really know how to converse on it. I am blithe; I will never have children

"Well, perhaps you're right," Mrs. Locke says mildly, and stuffs the holograms back into her evening bag. "My, how serious we've gotten from pretty young Tasha's dancing! Was I right to think she fluffed the second-act supported promenade, or is that just my old eyes?"

I breathe easier; this is better conversation. "Yes, she did. But usually she's very good."

"Well, I suppose nobody's at the top of their form all the time. Although you seem to be; I've never seen you give a bad performance." She smiles, both admiring and just a touch shy.

"Thank you."

"I've watched you for years, you know, whenever I visit my son in Washington. It's you that convinced me that the great Balanchine was wrong."

"When he said 'Dance is woman'?"

"Dance is muscle and bone, and male dancers have more of both."

I can't help it; I laugh aloud. From across the Promenade, Melita smiles approvingly.

Mrs. Locke says, "I've enjoyed talking to you tremendously, Cameron, and I know I mustn't monopolize you. But I do have one last question, if I may."

"Go ahead," I say, because despite myself, I like her.

She puts her hand on my arm. "I was in Washington last winter on an extended visit. Fun, but still, you know how family can be if you're there for half a year. I'd hoped to escape any little squabbles by watching you dance. But I went to every performance at Aldani House from January to April, and you didn't appear once. Why not?"

I freeze. Those were the months of my memory operation, plus whatever . . . happened before the operation. I never think about it, if I can help it.

Mrs. Locke's eyes are bonded to my face. She says, "Oh, dear—you don't want to talk about it."

"No," I say. "I was . . . ill."

"I understand. I'm sorry to have asked, since obviously it's something that has upset you. Clearly you don't talk about it with anybody."

"No."

"Not even your nearest and dearest?" she says, with a sudden arch glance at Rob, and it's so obvious that she's trying for a lighthearted tone, trying to make me feel better, that I feel a rush of sudden warmth. She really is a nice old lady.

"No, not even with my nearest and dearest." I try to match her tone. "Nor my farthest and feared."

"I can't believe *you* have any of those."

"You'd be surprised," I say, and it comes out not as lighthearted as I'd hoped, so I add jocularly, "There's always the wild fans breaking down doors to get to me."

"And you don't tell them anything either?"

"Especially not them," I say, and because I'm thinking of the soldier at International Center just a few days after the attack on Rob and me in the alleyway, it doesn't come out sounding jocular at all.

Mrs. Locke looks puzzled, and watches my face, and waits. Again I don't know what to say next. In fact, the whole conversation seems to have collapsed. Damn Melita; I'm just not *good* at talking to outsiders. But the silence lengthens, so I blurt out, "Just recently a fan actually broke into my dressing room at the International Center. It was a little unnerving. She was armed. But Security is very good about such things, and they got her."

"Goodness! And you've never seen her since?"

"No," I say, grateful for that. Maybe the girl soldier is still in jail. I hope so.

Mrs. Locke nods, and because she sees I'm distressed, she stands up and puts out her hand. "Again, wonderful to actually meet you. I'm such an admirer of yours, Cameron. Take care of yourself, now." And she walks away, to spare me any more dumb embarrassment. She really is a kind person.

I also stand, stretch, and look at Melita. She nods. I've done my part; I can go. Gratefully, I disappear downstairs, where Rob is waiting.

That night, I dream again, the first time in a while. I am poking through the debris of a ruined house, heavily overgrown with weeds. In a growth of ferns beside a broken concrete wall I find a nest of human babies. Each is grossly deformed: one has the arms of a dog, another the head of a bat. I back away, but the babies all suddenly rise in a cloud and fasten small sharp teeth into my skin all over my body.

I shriek and try to yank them off; they don't budge. Their animal eyes watch me unblinkingly. Rob shakes me awake.

"Cam! Cam!"

"Oh . . . I . . . oh . . ."

"You were dreaming again." He folds his arms around me. "Another animal dream?"

"Yes," I gasp.

"Genetic hybrids, again?"

"Yes."

He rubs my back, kisses my head. "Cam, darling, I looked it all up in the library banks. Remember? Those things can't exist. Even if the government allowed it, we just don't have the science to splice DNA like that. Nobody in the world does. All the scientists agree on that."

"I know." The words come out muffled against his shoulder. I could feel my heart calming.

"I think you should call Dr. Newell and have her increase your patch medication again."

"No. No, Rob, I can't." Too high dosage slows my reaction time. Not much, only a fraction of a second, most people wouldn't even notice. But I am a dancer. A fraction of a second matters.

"All right," Rob says. He's already drifting back to sleep. My next question wakes him again, even though it's whispered in the dark.

"Rob . . . when we make love, and I touch you . . . there are ridges of skin on my balls. Scars. But not on yours. Why?"

His body tenses. "Cameron, love . . . don't ask."

"No memory operation should give me scars on my balls."

"Please don't ask."

I don't. But it is a long time before I can go back to sleep. Tomorrow I'll be sluggish at morning class. And it's Tuesday; Mr. C. himself, not Rebecca, leads class on Tuesdays and Thursdays. I *can't* be sluggish.

But I am. Mr. C. gazes at me thoughtfully—a bad sign. Tasha's dancing is still off. Eric Carter and Sarah are still pointedly ignoring each other; Dmitri still mooning after Vivian Vargas; Laura still upset, biting her full underlip. Joaquim, sidelined for at least two weeks, watches forlornly, his knee propped on a chair. It's not a good class.

And afterwards, Melita stops me in the shabby, cheerless lounge area understage. She's icy. "Cameron, I checked on your patron of last night, Justine Locke. No record of her anywhere. No wonder she only made her request an hour before the performance—she knew I wouldn't have time to do a background check."

"She lied?" I say stupidly.

"She lied. Just another crazy fan willing to cheat to get to talk for half an hour to a dancer. And you gave her what she wanted." Melita rustles indignantly down the hallway, as if the disappointment of Mrs. Locke were *my* fault.

I'll be glad when we return to Washington, and Aldani House.

10

NICK CLEMENTI

The morning I left for Atlanta to visit my daughter Sallie, it seemed that I might not even get as far as the airport. I had to stop often to rest as I showered, dressed, packed. And the phone didn't stop ringing. Committee business, friendship business, business business. The only people I didn't talk to were Maggie and Vanderbilt Grant.

I was glad not to talk to Maggie—in fact, I had arranged it that way. She was spending three days with her sister in Louisville. The morning she'd left, I'd gone again to the hospital for another outpatient treatment. They'd cleared out the latest diseased tissues from my sinuses, where mucormycosis begins. They'd put more patches with more antifungals and blood-sugar stabilizers under my skin. They'd done a brain scan. I declined to hear the results. I didn't want Maggie questioning me yet, either. I'd tell her at the right time, my time. *It was not Death, for I stood up, / And all the dead lie down—*

Emily Dickinson.

But Van's silence was troubling. He hadn't sent me the promised information about FBI records on Cameron Atuli. Was that because he had found nothing—or because he had? Either way, this trip to Atlanta was designed to speed Van Grant along.

I was finally ready to leave for the airport when John called. "Dad?"

"Yes, John. Look, can I call you back later from—"

"This is an emergency."

The words no parent ever wants to hear. John's face looked haggard. I felt for the chair behind me. "Go on."

"It's Laurie. She's having some sort of breakdown."

"Where is she? Have you called a doctor?"

"She doesn't need a *doctor*, Dad! That's your solution to everything! This is different, dammit!"

I held onto my temper. "Just tell me what happened, John."

"She hasn't stopped crying for two days. Ever since the Goldstones—our neighbors—had their baby. Laurie went to see the baby, came home, and started to cry. And hasn't stopped." His voice turned slightly aggrieved. "It hasn't been easy around here."

I tried to picture Laurie—sunny, tender Laurie—sobbing for two days, and my chest hurt. "What can I do, John?"

"Talk to her, Dad. She always listens to *you*."

"Of course I'll talk to her, if you think it will help. But right now I have to leave for the airport, my plane takes off in a little over an hour, and—"

"I'll send Laurie to the airport to talk to you there."

This didn't strike me as a good plan. A crowded waiting area or bar, time pressing in, Laurie in tears . . . Something else struck me. "What do you mean, 'send' her? Won't you bring her yourself?"

"I can't. I have a job interview."

Deep breath. Don't lose composure. At thirty-six, John wasn't going to stop shifting responsibility whenever he could. Not unless Laurie actually left him, God forbid.

I said, "Let me talk to Laurie."

"I'll get her."

A delay, and then Laurie's voice, thick but not hysterical. "Dad? Thanks for agreeing to meet me at the airport. I appreciate it, when I know how busy you are."

So John had taken choice out of my hands. I said, "Never too busy for you, Laurie." If I had to, I'd rebook my flight to Atlanta. Sallie would understand. "Do you know where the Wright Bar is at National? In Terminal A?"

"Yes." She was trying hard to sound normal.

"I'll be there in half an hour."

"Thank you, Dad," she said, sounding suddenly, and uncharacteristically, like a little girl. I broke the link before I had to talk again to John, gathered my bag, and started for the door. I almost made it when the wall screen brightened and Shana's beautiful heartless face appeared.

"Hi, Nick. This is prerecorded. You're probably leaving for the airport right now, so I'll be quick. I won't be home for a few days. I'm visiting some NS buddies in Philly. Don't worry, I'll be back for my hearing, I won't stick you with bail. Everything's fine." And she winked.

I wanted to strangle her. Undoubtedly she wasn't visiting NS buddies, wasn't in Philadelphia, and might not make the hearing. God knows what she was really doing. But there was no time to do anything about it now—as she well knew.

That some people can't reproduce may be an evolutionary advantage for the race as a whole.

As I hobbled through the airport, my right eye ached, even as my vision seemed to have sharpened. I noticed everything:

The number of wheelchairs, most occupied.

The rapidly disappearing stack of large-print newspapers. The young prefer their news on the net.

The proud young mother in a corner chair, breastfeeding discreetly but not too discreetly, enjoying the envious glances of others.

The ten-year-old throwing a tantrum because his father wouldn't allow him to climb onto a high railing.

The toddler with vacant, staring eyes.

The bright lighting, so much brighter than in my youth. The old may have as few as ten percent of their original retinal cones.

The proudly pregnant woman, who may or may not understand that she has nearly a twenty-five percent chance of miscarriage.

I noticed these things, but the Committee would not. Not consistently, not all at the same time, not as part of a pattern. They refused to notice.

We had been throwing synthetic chemicals into the world for two hundred years, and for nearly a hundred of them, people had worried about those chemicals causing cancer. But nobody got cancer anymore. The medical techniques for bio-isolating, surrounding, and shutting down tumors were too good. Cancer had been conquered, and in a country with severe financial and demographic crises, nobody wanted to believe that those pesky chemicals weren't completely conquered as well. Public attention had moved on.

But the chemicals that disrupted animal endocrine systems had not. In the body such chemicals break down slowly, or not at all. Researchers of course knew this, but in times of scaled-back basic research, it was not a medical priority. People, after all, were not dying of this. People were staying healthy and strong.

Except—fetuses are not exactly people. Even infants are far from neurologically formed. They're people-in-progress, and a tiny dose of a synthetic chemical that fit into an endocrine receptor, a dose an adult body wouldn't even notice, can cause profound consequences in the womb. Or in the developing infant. For some endocrine disrupters, a dose of two parts per billion would do it. And most disrupters carry so easily on the wind. In two hundred years they had come to blanket the globe with astonishing evenness.

The proud young mother giving her baby breast milk, here or in Brazil, was also giving it huge doses of synthetic endocrine disrupters. They accumulated in body fat, especially at the top of the food chain, and breast milk was heavily fatty.

The ten-year-old having a tantrum, here or in Jakarta, may or may not have neurological impairment or a learning disability. Endocrine disrupters affect the brain.

The vacant-eyed toddler, here or in London, was only one statistic on the sharp upswing of birth defects. In the womb, timing is all. A small dose of endocrine disrupters can cause even the best genetic blueprint to be built wrong.

The pregnant mother, here or in Tokyo, who suffers a miscarriage—nowadays, one in four—will never know what caused it. Nor will the childless couple, here or in Melbourne, who spend years and fortunes and heartbreak trying to conceive. Nothing in your environment, the doctors tell them, has such an effect under laboratory conditions. Nothing we could have done, my dear—just nature taking its course, I'm so sorry. If anything chemical could produce such an effect, it would of course be instantly taken off the market. FDA tests are more thorough than ever. All environmental chemicals are thoroughly vetted.

But no one tests them *in combination*. It just isn't possible. There are thousands of endocrine-disrupting chemicals, which means billions of possible permutations. And that's even before you realize that for some disrupters, tests to measure small-enough doses don't even exist.

Or before you consider the complex feedback loops one endocrine disrupter can set up for another. Endocrine disrupters, endocrine blockers, endocrine-disrupter blockers, all behaving differently for each synthetic. Testing is a hopeless idea.

Or before you realize that disruption can occur in many different ways: by mimicking natural hormones and binding to their receptors. By blocking natural hormones from binding to their receptors. By reacting directly with hormones. By altering patterns of natural hormone synthesis. By disturbing distribution of natural receptor sites . . . or any of those in combination.

So why attack what is hopeless to solve? Why publicize what you can't, for ethical reasons, replicate in the laboratory? Why bother with controls impossible to justify, enforce, or drum up support for? Synthetic chemicals are in everything we touch every day. Why uselessly anger their manufacturers and users (no industry would remain untouched)? Why anger women (just one more thing mother can be blamed for)? There was, after all, no conclusive hard proof.

"Dad?"

After all, it's not as if DNA were being tampered with. And the fall in sperm count *is* leveling off; maybe it will rebound. Mother Nature is resourceful. Human reproduction is infinitely resilient, infinitely adaptable.

Yes. Right. As were the dinosaurs.

"Dad?"

Laurie stood beside me in front of the Wright Bar. She wore one of those new hats, a sort of abbreviated helmet with a holo veil that made even plain features look soft and mysterious. The veil was turned up full strength. I was shocked to see how much thinner she'd gotten. Taking her arm, I led her to the farthest corner of the bar, in shadows. Holos of Kitty Hawk planes swooped above us, disappeared before they hit the far wall.

"Turn off your hat, Laurie. I don't care if you've been crying."

Reluctantly, she blanked the holo. Laurie wasn't pretty the same way Shana was pretty, and now she looked almost ugly. Too gaunt; she'd lost so much weight. Strong square jaw, splotchy skin, small eyes too close together and, now, red and swollen. But the expression in those eyes had always seemed to me the sweetest I'd ever seen. Laurie was that rarity, a completely good person, without pettiness or malice. *Far above rubies is her price.* . . . I took Laurie's thin hand. "Tell me, sweetheart. What is it?"

She just shook her head, the tears starting again.

"John said you went to see your neighbors' new baby."

"Yes," she said, and I saw the Herculean effort to control herself. Laurie's feelings ran deep. "I'm being a stewdee, Dad, I know. But I've tried and tried to accept that John and I will never have . . . I know millions of other couples are in the same boat. I know we're nothing special. Only . . ."

"You'll always be special, Laurie."

". . . only I can't seem to stop *crying.*"

"Would you consider medication, honey?"

"I've already got patches for Serentil and Alixolin."

Both were strong and reliable neurotransmitter adjusters, and they weren't helping. There are griefs that go beyond pharmacology. "Laurie, what can I—"

"Find me a baby to adopt."

She might as well have asked for a mastodon to domesticate. Unless she meant . . .

"Find a baby how, honey? Here, order something to drink, you'll feel better."

She keyed in something on the table order pad; I don't think she herself knew what. I ordered wine, even though it would upset my insulin bio-monitors. Mucor likes sugar-rich blood.

"Find a baby how, Laurie? John told me you'd ransacked the adoption nets, and—"

"On the black market. A baby on the black market."

Now that she'd actually said it, she suddenly calmed down. Making the decision had been wracking her. Laurie—like Sallie and Maggie—believed in law, in playing fair, in the social contract. I knew, as she did not, that she wouldn't last a week on the black market.

"Laurie, honey . . . even if I knew how to do that, and even if you were willing to risk the legal penalties, it's unbelievably expensive, and besides—"

"We'll give everything. Every penny. We'll pledge future earnings." She leaned forward eagerly, the tears gone. "Anything at all!"

"Does John agree with that?" I couldn't see John, always so solicitous of his own comforts, going along with this.

"He doesn't know yet that I'm thinking about the . . . the black market. But when he does, I'm sure he'll agree. He wants a child as much as I do. Oh, Dad, you don't know how it is! I wake up in the morning, and I hear the Goldstone baby through the window, and my arms just curve around an empty space. I walk around with an empty place in my chest, all day, every day—a physical hole. I can't sleep, can't eat, can't concentrate. Sometimes it gets so bad that it physically hurts to *move*, to put one foot in front of the other and get on with it. And I can't stop *crying*. I know not all women are like this, and I tell myself that nobody gets everything and I should be grateful for what I do have, and to forget all about motherhood, but . . . but I can't. I *can't*. And it feels like I never will!"

I believed her. In some women, the maternal instinct is so strong that its thwarting creates a sorrow that never heals. Nothing in the human genome data justifies this in terms of DNA or proteins. But it is nonetheless so.

"We'll pay anything for a baby, Dad! Everything!"

"Honey, your and John's everything is still so much less than the really rich can pay, and there are so few babies even on the black market—"

"But you're a doctor! And you have contacts on the Hill, in the whole scientific world, everywhere! You can find us a child in ways no one else we know possibly could!"

Her plain, honest face glowed with trust. I looked away.

"Laurie, even if that were true—"

"And you and Mom want a grandchild, I know you do. Oh, Dad, this means so much. To me it means everything. I don't care about the risk of legal penalties. Please don't say no. We've always depended on you, the whole family, to do everything, and I know it's not fair to you, but for this . . ." Her voice broke. "Please try."

And I couldn't refuse. Not Laurie. Not when I was going to leave them all so soon, without me to depend on any more. Hubris? Yes. *Pride goeth* . . . but pride didn't exist any more, not officially. Only shared responsibility.

"All right, honey," I said. "I'll try."

"Thank you," she said simply, with a curious humble dignity, as if all the previous histrionics were somehow unworthy of the enormous pledge being given. I didn't like that. It mattered to her so much; what if I failed?

The table suddenly said pleasantly, "Final boarding call for Flight 164 to Atlanta. You are registered as a passenger on that flight."

I'd forgotten that I'd given the system my credit number to pay for our drinks. I stood, too suddenly, and then pretended to stretch in order to cover the trembling in my legs. "That's my flight, Laurie."

"I'll walk you to the gate," she said, her face luminous now, so that despite her swollen red eyes, men turned to look after her as we passed. I tried to match her eager young stride, and hoped that when she made her way back out of the airport alone, the nursing mother would have already left.

Atlanta had rain, sheets of it, slabs of it. Before I could stop myself, I started ticking off all the synthetic, windborne disrupters that were probably coming down with each drop. Hexachlorobenzene, kelthane, octochlorostyrene, the alkyl phenols . . . I told myself to cut it out and pay attention to my reason for being here.

Sallie met me at the airport. She was looking older—with a shock I realized that she was almost fifty. Born when Maggie, I, and the world had all seemed young.

"Dad! You're looking marvelous!"

"Liar."

"Well, sort of marvelous." She grinned. Neither of our daughters got Maggie's looks—those all went to John. Alana, on Mars Colony Three for ten years now, looked like me. Sallie looked like herself: big, cheerful, noisy, direct. She'd been at the CDC for fifteen years, and loved her work, her husband, her life.

"So what's all the mystery about this visit?" she said as we pulled away from the airport. Sallie was an exciting driver; I steadied myself against the seat. Her car, I noted, was not driver-enhanced; it featured none of the expensive options to allow the aged rich to keep driving. No virtual reality screen to compensate for dimming vision. No augmented field of view for necks that could no longer swivel easily. No smart computer to assume decision making for slowed reaction times. Sallie's car was just a car. But, then, Sallie was barely fifty.

She said, "Why are you here for just a few hours? Richard will be sorry to miss you. And what's so secret that you couldn't tell me about it on the phone?"

"A favor," I said. "I need a large favor from you, Sallie. Head out to the CDC."

At my tone, she glanced sideways at me. Rain poured down the windshield. Sallie swerved from lane to lane. "Am I free to say no? Your tone doesn't seem to allow much room for that."

"I hope you won't say no."

"What is it?"

I gathered myself together. "I need a list of CDC vivifacture cell donors, both voluntary and involuntary."

She said automatically, "You know I can't do that."

"I know you can. I'm asking if you will."

We drove in silence for several minutes, rain pounding on the roof. Sallie has an expressive face. I watched her ethics wrestle with her curiosity, her family loyalty with her natural conformity. I didn't interrupt. Finally she said, "Why?"

The opening wedge. Once curiosity is uppermost, you can bargain to keep it there. "I can't tell you that. But I guarantee that the information will not be used in any way that will compromise the CDC, or will be in any way traceable back to you. And I'm only looking for one specific name, if that makes it any easier for you to break security."

"It does," she said, which of course I'd counted on. "Who?"

"Cameron Atuli. A-T-U-L-I." The name meant nothing to Sallie; she wasn't a ballet type.

"ID number?"

"I don't know. But he's a male in his twenties, residing in Washington."

Sallie sighed. She didn't like this. But if it was only one name, and only for her father, the most trustworthy of men . . . she was as transparent as air.

As some air. Rain still streamed down, with its invisible burdens.

"All right, Dad. I'll look. But only because I know you won't do anything wrong or unethical with the information."

"Thank you, Sallie." I knew better than to ask her help with Laurie; Sallie might filch information but never babies.

"Technically, the CDC doesn't even have any interest in vivifacture," Sallie said heavily. "We don't keep deebees on it. We're too busy with falling sperm count."

"I know," I said, and we both smiled at the irony. Falling sperm count is not exactly a disease. No one is sick with it. The NIH and the national laboratories could work on fertility, of course, as part of their mandate into general research (they could also work on vivifacture). The FDA was supposed to investigate and certify all "cures" for low sperm count; that was one way Vanderbilt Grant exercised his considerable power. In theory, the CDC was supposed to confine itself to disease. In practice, the last twenty years had turned its "public health" mandate into the medical arm of the Justice Department, who otherwise could not combat esoteric medical crimes it didn't remotely understand. The result was constant turf wars, made worse by constantly shrinking funding. Hard to believe that once, Congress routinely committed over a hundred billion dollars annually to science.

And some CDC databases were completely unknown to almost everyone. Computers off the net, within shielded and secure rooms, available only to senior people with proper clearances. Like Sallie.

"Stay in the car," she said when we arrived at the CDC facility. "I'll be about half an hour."

She was longer. Chatting with colleagues? Sallie was not a good poker player. I sat and watched the rain slacken, stop, start again harder than ever. Whenever it rained this hard in Bethesda, the stream behind my house overflowed. With the overflow came a sudden visibility of frogs. Frogs, spending much of their time in water, were like miners' canaries: sensitive to environmental changes. My backyard overflow delivered frogs with one leg, frogs with withered legs, frogs with clubfoot-legs, frogs with no legs. A Frenchman would be gastronomically deprived next to my stream.

Finally Sallie, dripping wet, climbed back into the car. She shook herself like a large, unhappy, faithful dog and didn't look at me directly.

"Well, Atuli's there, all right. Dad, what *is* this about? You picked yourself a scary one."

"Scary?" I hadn't expected that.

"No, on second thought, I don't want to know. I'll tell you what I discovered, and then we won't mention this at lunch, or ever again. Okay?"

"Okay," I said. Rain streamed off her hair onto her broad forehead. She swiped at it ineffectually.

"Cameron Atuli's cells are indeed in the library, as an involuntary donor. Stratum lucidum, stratum basale, dermis, sebaceous glands—all of it, everything needed to grow skin grafts. The source is listed as the FBI, which means they were seized during a raid on an illegal medical operation. You don't look surprised."

"I guess I'm not," I said. "But there's more, isn't there?"

"There is indeed," she said grimly. "No internal-organ cells are in the library—except one. Testicles."

"*Testicles?*"

"Yes. And a note that the cells are fertile. Cameron Atuli has a sperm count of three hundred million per liter of semen."

Three hundred million. My God.

"Or rather, *had.* After I found that, I cross-checked the deebee for government hospital admissions near the date of the cell donation. Atuli was a patient at Carter Memorial, and he was assigned heavy security. The operation was a testicular implant. That's to simulate the appearance of testicles and scrotum when they've been horribly damaged, or when a child is born without. The operation—"

"I know what it is," I said, too irritably. Trying to assimilate it all. A testicular implant is, of course, infertile, although it can produce normal ejaculation.

"I wasn't going to explain the operation," Sallie said, equally irritably. "To *you?* Come on. I was going to add that the testicular implant was followed by induced retrograde amnesia."

So young Cameron Atuli wouldn't even remember his . . . what? Abduction, perhaps. Involuntarily cell donation. Hours immobile in the MOSS tank, terrified for his life, followed by castration . . . dancers, like all creative people, tended to be a little unstable to begin with. The induced amnesia was probably a mercy operation. Authorized by whom? Paid for by whom?

"One more piece of information, because I know you're going to ask," Sallie said. She stared rigidly ahead. "Yes, I looked through all the deebees available to me. That's what took so long. And no, the CDC does not possess Cameron Atuli's fertile testicles. And now don't ever ask me to do anything like this again, Dad."

She looked so miserable: wet, bedraggled, guilty, concerned. But Sallie was resilient—as the more vulnerable Laurie was not. "I won't ask you ever again," I promised.

"Good. Now let's go to lunch."

On the flight home, I tried to think it through. The FBI had made a raid and interrupted an illegal vivifacture lab in the process of raping Cameron Atuli's cells. At least part of the process, the MOSS tank readings and initial cultures, had been completed and some cells shipped to another location. I knew that because finished skin grafts later turned up on Shana's chimps. Skin and related cell samples that remained in the illegal lab ended up at the CDC, as usual. But the severed testicles had not. Had they, too, been shipped to the warehouse in Lanham before the FBI raid, and had they been blown to smithereens in the train-wreck explosion? Or had the man that Shana had seen carrying the chimps also been carrying Cameron Atuli's fertile balls?

And where *was* Shana? Was that wretched little witch going to skip bail after all?

Suddenly I was sick of thinking about it all. I was a physician, not a detective. A doctor who was dying. That's where my energies should be going— into deciding how to tell Maggie and the children, into finishing my estate planning to leave them as comfortable as I could. Into doing the last thing well that I could do well. *If I must die/ I will encounter darkness as a bride/ And hug it in my arms. . . .* Shakespeare.

We had flown above the storm. I stared out the window at the gray clouds below, and tried to think what to say to Maggie, due back tomorrow from her sister's.

But at home I was sidetracked again. There was a message from Van Grant, voice and visual both:

"Sorry to take so long to get back to you, Nick, on that matter we discussed the other day. But I wanted to be as thorough as possible. I had my people check every government deebee in existence—all of them. No unusual activity for the person you mentioned, in any way, ever."

He spread his hands helplessly and smiled regretfully from the wall screen, the smile I'd known for fifty years: warm, sincere, trustworthy. "Sorry, Nick. But isn't it nice to know that at least one citizen is leading a completely normal life? Wish *I* were." An appealing chuckle. "Take care, Nick. My love to Maggie. Helen and I hope to see you two again real soon."

The screen blanked. My eye hurt, and my cheek; a sore was developing inside my mouth. And I was suddenly bone-weary—with age, with mucormycosis, with stress, with lies. All I wanted was to go to sleep, the sooner the better, and the only thing that kept me from bed at five in the afternoon was that I'd have to lie shivering there without Maggie, alone.

11

SHANA WALDERS

New York is a dead town.

I don't mean there isn't no action. There's lots of action, if you don't mind ending up pretty dead yourself. And at the other end, there's lots of safe, high-toned, boring action: swank parties, thee-ay-ter, opera, charity balls. I know because from the minute I get off the train, I make it my business to know. But what New York don't got is exciting-not-stupid middle action, for a gorgeous kid like me. Or at least I don't find it. But then I think maybe that's just as well, because that's not what I'm here for anyway. And dressed like a dirty boy, with my hair stuffed under a helmet and my clothes droopy as an old dick, I don't look so gorgeous anyway.

By eight o'clock it's getting dark, but New York still shells out enough money to light the outside of Lincoln Center, and anyway there's an almost-full moon. I fit right into the crowd hanging around the dried-up fountain, doing deals and sucking sunshine and panhandling the dressed-up stewdees going to the ballet. But unlike most of the crowd, I'm clean and sober and wearing a pair of cheap zooms that make everything up close look blurry but everything a hundred yards away sharp as needles.

The New York State Theater has a front all of glass. It's streaky and spotty. Some guy told me there used to be curtains to give the rich people some privacy, but now they don't got enough money (who does?) and so I can see inside, even through the dirt, to where the party is. At least, I can see the things closest to the glass. The lights inside don't burn nowhere near as bright as the blinders safeguarding the outside from scum like us.

With my zooms I can see little tables with fancy food and vases of flowers. I can see Cameron Atuli, still in his rucky-fucky dance costume, sitting on a marble bench close to the window. And I can see the little old lady who talks to him for a long, long time. Except for his lover, she's the only one who does.

When the party's over, I follow her. The dealer at the fountain told me the party's for rich people who might give the ballet some money, and this little old lady looks like a rich person. But she don't *smell* right to me. I don't know how to explain it. She just didn't talk to nobody but Atuli, she left right after that, and her whole body, from a hundred yards away, just looks too . . . smooth-walking. Too disciplined. Too *young*.

She crosses the fountain square real near me, accompanied by one of the bruisers that Lincoln Center hires to escort rich people to their cars or cabs. She passes right next to me. But I can't take the zooms out without looking conspicuous, and she isn't nothing but a smeary blur. But when she gets farther away, I see the escort put her into a cab, and I take off after it, a safe distance behind, on a powerboard I snaggled in the park. Following the cab is easy; New York traffic can't move for shit.

She gets out at a fairly nice, secure apartment building on West End Avenue. I note the address and go home, which is a friend's place. He's not a close friend, but he'll let me

stay there as long as I want, for the usual bonus. I hope it's
not too long. He's a nice-enough guy, but in bed he just
don't know what he's doing, and I'm not interested in
teaching him.

The next morning I'm back at West End Avenue real
early, panhandling out past the secure zone. The guard
glares at me but legally there isn't nothing he can do. About
7:30 my bitch comes out, only she don't look exactly the
same. Thirty years younger, dressed in a business suit with
a plain vest, but it's still her all right. Today no cab; she
takes the subway, and I follow along.

She goes all the way to an office building downtown. I
don't go in, but I don't need to. From outside I can see the
little sign on the lobby wall: Federal Bureau of Investigation.

Well, well.

Next I go hang around the back doors to the New York
State Theater. The terminal I accessed in the Lincoln Center Library—and I never smelled such a stinking library,
they just got hardly nobody throwing out homeless fos-
sils—said that's where the practice rooms for ballet are.
The building don't have any restaurant. Everybody's got to
eat sometime.

But not alone. I don't expect that, not after what happened to him in Washington with Dreamie and Teela.
Atuli's got with him not only his lover but a bunch of
other dancers, six of them altogether, men and women,
going out for lunch. I'm only going to get one shot.

I wait till they're standing in line at a restaurant on Am-
sterdam, relaxed and talking. "Mr. Atuli? Could I talk with
you for a minute?"

I still look like a panhandler, but I'm careful to speak well, and I don't stand too close. Still, Atuli takes a step backward and his lover says, "Go away. Now."

"I know you're Cameron Atuli," I say, "but I'm not a crazy fan." Yecchhh. "I have some information you really want to know. About your operation."

That gets his attention. It's sort of a shot in the sky, but not really. Those chimps had his face; there must of been *some* sort of operation, sometime, to make that happen. I don't plan to get too specific yet. Let him think I know a lot more than I do.

But he don't react like I hoped. "I don't want to know anything about it!" he says, and backs away. Two other dancers step in front of him, and another one starts looking around for a surveillance cam or a cop.

So I'm cornered, and I've only got about twenty seconds. I say, loud enough for him to hear from behind his friends, "I saw the chimps with your face! That's why I tried to get to you in the International Center! To warn you!" And I pull off my hat so all my blond hair tumbles out, and raise my face so he can see under the filth that I'm not no old bum.

"Go! Now!" his lover shouts and starts shoving me. I didn't know a rucky-fucky dancer could be so strong. People are stopping on the sidewalk now, to look: so many young people in one place, fighting. Down the street I see a cop on his powerboard. The dancer shoves me even farther away, and this time another one helps him. A girl pulls Atuli's arm toward the restaurant door.

It's over. I crashed it.

But then Atuli, who's been shrinking away from me like

I stink of shit, breaks from the girl and pushes over to me. "What chimps?"

"Cam, don't listen to her!"

"No, wait, Joaquim, let her go. Sarah, let go of me! You—what chimps?"

"Cam, *don't*—"

"Hush, Rob. Please. There shouldn't have been any chimps in my . . . you. How did you even know I'd had an operation? Who . . . who are you?"

A second chance. I pull free of the dancers, who stand around scowling, and face Atuli respectfully. The cop on the board cruises past.

"I know you had an operation because I saw the result—your face on three live monkeys. Only nobody don't believe me. And I'm betting you didn't do it willing, and that you want to know more about it!" Did he? From his face — God, up close he was beautiful, too bad all the prettiest ones are blithe—I couldn't tell. Mostly he looked scared.

"Chimps? But how . . . ?"

"Stop, Cameron. Now," his lover says quietly. "This is why you had the operation."

There's a long moment where nobody says nothing, and you couldn't of dented the air with a lasersaw.

Then Atuli says, "You're right, Rob. Miss, whoever you are—just leave me alone." He turns toward the restaurant.

"But I saw them! With your face!" I shout, like an idiot. A dancer gives me a final shove and I sprawl on the sidewalk. The last of them disappears into the restaurant. They can have the law here in minutes.

I pick myself up and sprint away. Damn it to fucking hell. Atuli don't care that somebody's been growing his own face and sticking it onto monkeys, to sell to weepy bitches desperate for anything they can pretend is a baby. He don't even care!

Why not?

Blocks away, gasping for air in a public toilet booth—since I left NS I just don't get no exercise—I think about Atuli's reactions. It was like he don't *know* about the chimps. How could that be? He was there, Nick told me all about how Atuli must of been inside some sort of machine for hours, and must of been awake, too, for the machine to work. So how come he don't know?

"Stop, Cameron. Now. This is why you had the operation."

A memory wipe.

I'd been hoping for information from somebody who's had all his information deleted. Who didn't know his own name until he learned it all over again. Some investigator I am!

I slump down on the toilet seat, ready to give up. Go back to Washington, go to my hearing (which I plan to do anyhow; Nick's been pretty decent to me, for a rusty fusty), take my slap on the wrist from the judge. And then what? Give up, forget the army, become a clerk someplace sitting in front of a screen all day transferring potatoes from one warehouse to another.

No. I'd die. I *have* to get into the army, and to do that I have to prove my story about the chimps is true. But Cameron Atuli don't remember about the chimps. So now what?

"Stop, Cameron. Now. This is why you had the operation."

His lover remembers. About whatever happened to Atuli that made him have his memory wiped. And maybe his lover knows where, or who, or something else I can follow up on to prove my story's true.

I straighten up and leave the toilet stall, which, now that I notice it, smells as bad as everything else in this city. I'll be glad to leave. The ballet bunch will be going back to Washington, too, next week. I'll have another shot there. This time, at Robert Radisson.

I get back to Washington forty minutes before the hearing, which goes real quick. I stand next to Nick, who might look like shit these days but is still important and rich. I wear a white dress I stole on the way to the courthouse. My hair is caught in a ribbon at the back of my head. I bow my head a little and speak soft. I try to look like an orphaned national resource who just needs a little guidance. The judge puts me on probation.

"You little fraud," Nick says outside the courthouse. He has to lean against the building wall. "Where have you been for three days?"

"New York," I say, and right away he gets it. He may be dying, but his brain works just fine.

"The Aldani Ballet is there on tour. You went to badger Cameron Atuli."

"And it didn't work," I say, even now hating to admit that. "He don't remember nothing. He had a memory wipe."

Nick don't react. He just says, "Are you certain? Tell me why you think so."

So I go through the whole story, leaving nothing out, telling it straight.

"FBI," Clementi says, like he's trying the idea out. But he

still don't look really surprised, which surprises *me*. He's
holding out on me.

"And what did *you* find out while I was gone, Nick?"

"Nothing," he says, and he's lying. Suddenly I'm furi-
ous—with him because I thought he was really on my side.
And with myself, for believing it for half a shitty second.
Nobody's on your side but you.

He says, "Let's go home."

So I can't show how furious I am, because he's still giving me a place to stay, and if I don't stay there I'll never find
out what else he knows that I don't. So I take his arm and
we start off slowly for the cab stand. His steps wobble. In
just the few days I've been gone, he's worse.

So what. This old fart don't matter to me. Let him die.

When we get home, Her Highness is back from visiting her
sister. Her suitcase clutters up the front hall. She takes one
look at Nick, leaning on my arm to even walk into the
apartment, and she goes still all over.

"Nick."

"Hello, Maggie. I'm glad you're back."

She don't answer, and they look at each other, and I
know it's time for me to leave. "I'm going out," I say, and
go back through the front door. Then I go around the
building, up the service elevator, and in through the delivery door. I got the code from the super the first day, for
the usual fee. I inch along the hall until I can see them re-
flected in the mirror over the fireplace, and can hear them
clearly.

She's sitting real close to him on the sofa, one hand on
his knee, the other just touching the back of his neck.
Every once in a while her fingers move a little in his hair.

"Since when?" he asks.

"Weeks now. I knew you'd tell me when you chose to."

"You never said, never indicated by so much as a look—"

She laughs, shaky. "Isn't that supposed to be my line, Nick? Only you indicated it with every look, every movement. Did you think I don't know you well enough, after fifty-five years, to know when you're dying?"

He pulls her closer. They're quiet a minute, and then he says a weird thing. "I want to do it well, Maggie. The only way I can face it is to believe I'm doing it well."

"I understand," she says, so low I barely catch it. "And you don't want my help."

"Not 'don't want'—'can't take.' Because then I wouldn't be doing it as well as I need to. Does that make sense?"

"About you, darling—yes, it makes sense to me." Which makes one of us.

He chuckles. "No going not gently, no raging against the dying of the light. That's for the young. No rage at all. But, Maggie—I do need your help. With things I may not be able to get done before I . . . before."

"Anything, love. What sorts of things?"

"Not what, who. Shana and Laurie."

"Laurie? You mean, about getting a baby however she can?"

He pulls a little away to look into her face. "Is there anything you don't already know about your family?"

"Their numbers are legion," Maggie says. "But I only guessed about Laurie. She spoke to you, I take it. And you pledged to do whatever is necessary." She stops, and I watch her face struggle with itself. "And I will, too. Just don't tell Sallie."

"Which brings me to Shana," he says, and the back of my neck tingles.

"Shana? What's that slutty little con artist got to do with Sallie?"

"I flew to Atlanta yesterday, on the shuttle. I asked Sallie to get me some information from the CDC deebees, and, reluctantly, she did. Shana went tearing off to New York on her own and came back with more. And Van Grant reported in. Maggie, something is very wrong. Cameron Atuli was abducted, forced to donate the tissue samples and MOSS scan that ended up creating the chimps that Shana saw. Atuli was also castrated, and his testicles are still with his abductors. The FBI rescued him. Afterwards he had a memory wipe, probably for the trauma. Sallie found some of this out in the top-security CDC deebees. But when Van called me, he said there was no mention of Atuli in any government deebee, anywhere. And I did a search in the public legal deebee myself. There's no court case, settled or pending, involving the kidnapping of Cameron Atuli. And Shana swears that a woman talking privately to Atuli in New York went to work the next day at the FBI."

Just in time, I keep from making a noise. Maggie don't. She grunts like he just hit her, and then she chokes out, "Do you know what you're saying, Nick? That Van—that the government—knows about a kidnapping, knows that criminals are making illegal monkey-human babies—or whatever they are—and isn't prosecuting!"

"There may be a reason. The Justice Department may be holding off because they're still tracing the operation to its roots."

"If that were so," Maggie argues, "they wouldn't have allowed a key witness like Atuli to have induced retrograde amnesia, no matter what his trauma. They'd need him to testify. Besides, the government isn't going to support animal/human vivifacture hybrids—no matter who wants a baby substitute! Half of the government is religious—"

"Ah, but which half? Van? He says so, but who knows what Vanderbilt Grant really believes?"

"—and *all* of the government knows that most people cringe from the idea of a chimp with a toddler's face. Or anything else like that. These are politicians, Nick—they're not going to allow, even covertly, something that polls show ninety percent of the voters abhor. There's no reason."

"I know," he says, and leans his head on the back of the sofa. His eye's twitching again. In the mirror I see Maggie's face, and I have to look away.

"Is it bad, dear heart?"

"No. No pain, not with the meds. But the mucor is growing into my brain, and I don't think it can be too long now before the coma. Laurie and Shana—you may have to finish helping both of them, Maggie."

"How?" she says, and I have to admit that the old bitch has class. She's not wailing and fussing and making it harder for him. She's like a platoon leader waiting for orders that she'll die herself trying to carry out, if he's the one giving them.

"I don't know. But Laurie needs—must have—a child. And Shana has to get accepted into the army. She's not suited for anything else."

"Why Shana?" Maggie says, somewhere between impatience and ice. "You've only known Shana a few weeks. She's a liar and a cheat. And she can take care of herself— she's been doing it for years. She's got her whole life ahead of her to get herself straightened out, if that's what she really wants. She's *young*, dearest. Why bother with Shana?"

"Because she's young," Nick says, and closes his eyes. Maggie lets her face go, then, and when I can't bear to watch it anymore in the mirror, I creep back along to the delivery door and jam the elevator between floors so I can be alone.

Maggie is right—Nick and me don't hardly know each other. Plus, he's a moldy oldie who already used up his share of time. Plus, he's one of the two generations that are breaking the backs of mine. Plus, he thinks I'm a waste of air, even if he is helping me get into the army. Probably hopes I'll get sent to South America and killed in action.

I know all that. But I'm crying anyway, slumped in my stupid white dress against the dirty service elevator wall, and I feel like the worst stewdee of all time.

12

CAMERON ATULI

The dreams about animals have ended. But now it's something worse.

It starts the day after that girl, the one who'd been the soldier in my dressing room in Washington, tries to attack us in New York. Rob and Joaquim and Dmitri keep her from touching me. But they can't stop her yelling, or me hearing: *I know you had an operation because I saw the result—your face on three chimps. . . . I saw them! With your face!*

"She's crazy," Rob says to me as we all crowd into the safety of the restaurant. Joaquim and Dmitri, Sarah and Caroline, say nothing. They're leaving it to Rob. But what do the other four know about what happened to me before my operation? What does that girl know? How much of my life is closed off from me—but not from everyone I live with, dance with, love with?

"I don't think I can go on like this," I say to Rob, before I know I'm going to. "Not knowing. That girl wasn't crazy, Rob—she didn't sound crazy." *Chimps with my face.*

"Not now," he says, glancing at the others, who are studying the menu screen as if they can't hear us. "Let's eat lunch."

And we do, discussing nothing but class, rehearsal, performance. I feel myself calm down. This is what matters, after all. Dancing. Nothing else.

But a week later, back in Washington, we start work on a new ballet, made on us by Mr. C. himself.

"Cameron, you and Sarah enter on diagonals, with *flick jetés* from opposite sides of the stage," he says. He demonstrates by crossing the practice room; at sixty, he still moves like a young man. In the sneakers, ugly pants, and red T-shirt he always wears at a first choreography session, he's almost like a parody of himself, except for his voice. It's strange to hear such decisive, brilliant direction in that flat, raspy Midwestern voice.

"Very energetic," he says. "You meet in the middle, *tendu croisé derrière*, look at each other and smile. Then Mitchell and Caroline repeat the movement, ending up *here.*"

I don't know why I'm supposed to be smiling at Sarah. I came in late—a great crime—and whatever Mr. C. has told the others about the ballet, he isn't repeating it to me. He's going to make me ask, as punishment.

I don't ask. I go through the entrance, and the combinations that follow. The music is aggressive, modern: Sabo, I guess, or Bolthouse. There are some very athletic, sexual moves for Sarah and me, Mitchell and Caroline. I decide we're two sets of lovers.

"Now, here," Mr. C. says, "the doctor enters, where the music breaks. Like this, Nicole. No, more stillness. You stand with your back to them, eight full beats, and the music delivers the verdict."

Doctor? Verdict?

"Now, Mitchell and Caroline, you sink to the floor, like this, overwhelmed. Sarah, you and Cameron have the counterpoint, the shock—but controlled, heavy, slow, to match the music. Watch—it's a short *pas de deux*, but an important one. Start with a supported arabesque third, and

Sarah you lean very far forward, you couldn't possibly maintain this position without his support and you know it . . . good. But drop your arm . . . that's good . . . Cameron, echo the forward yearning reach of her arm."

The little *pas de deux* is beautiful: intricate and moving, perfectly balanced. I can barely follow the steps. My chest is tight enough to hurt. Doctor? Verdict?

"You both exit stage right," Mr. C. says, "and Mitchell, you carry Caroline out stage left. Then, Sarah, you enter again, far to the rear, on the beat, slow sad *bourées*, conspicuously unsupported . . . no, dear, like *this*. Better. Now you freeze, *tendu effacé*, as the first of the unborn children flits across the stage in rapid *bourées*, head down."

Unborn children.

"You raise your head, Sarah, and when the music shifts—here—"

"Stop," I say, very loud. Everyone looks at me. "I came in late. Please, what is the ballet about?"

Mr. C. says nothing. One of his most infuriating habits is that he never repeats explanations; other dancers must do it for him. Sarah rushes in.

"It's about infertility, Cam. Both couples are trying to conceive, but can't, and then they're haunted by the shades of the children they'll never have—you know, a reverse on all those Romantic ballets where the principals are haunted by the shades of their dead—until near the end—"

"No," I say. "*No.*"

Sarah gapes at me.

"*No.* I won't dance it!"

There's an electric silence. I don't know what's wrong with me. My heart pounds so hard it fills my ears. I'm light-headed, as if I might faint.

"Dmitri," Mr. C. says calmly, "take Cameron's place."
Dmitri, watching the rehearsal, looks startled and moves
slowly next to Sarah. Mr. C. turns to me.

"Go to Melita," he says kindly. "Tell her you feel ill and
need to see Dr. Newell."

"I don't feel ill," I argue, further astonishing myself. "I
feel . . ." What? Why can't I dance this ballet?

"Go see Melita," Mr. C. says, and turns back to work. I
see that he's saving me face, giving me an excuse to leave
and also one to return later ("Dr. Newell says I'm fine.").
But I can't do it. I know suddenly that I can't dance this
ballet. Why not? I don't particularly care about children,
born or unborn. I never have. It makes no difference. I
can't dance the ballet. My body will not let me.

I rush out of the room.

In another, deserted practice room, I calm and center
myself, standing for a long time in the middle of the floor
with my head bent, concentrating as hard as I can. Then I
start a combination from *Sorrows*. *Tour en l'air, plié, relevé*,
and into the arabesque . . .

I stumble, my timing off. No, not my timing . . . something else. Some inner sureness about the flow of the steps,
about the space I should be carving into sharp sections,
about myself . . .

I try again.

And again.

I try the second act entrance from *Jupiter*, then my solo
from *Le Corsair*. I can't dance it, not any of it. I can make
my body go through the steps, but I can't *dance* it. From the
corner of my eye I see ghostly children *bourée*-ing across
the stage, and they're all chimps with my faces. No, I don't
see them. They're not there. But the thought of them is

there, gnawing at a part of my brain I don't even have any more, like the phantom pain of amputees. Or maybe that's not it. Whatever it is, I can't dance.

I can't dance.

I can't dance.

Rob sits on his bed in his room, sewing ribbons on shoes. I burst in and grab his shoulders. "Tell me!"

"Cam, what—"

"Tell me now! Everything that happened to me before the operation!"

He says, with forced steadiness, "You don't want to know."

"No, I don't! But I have to, because it keeps coming back to jolt me every way I turn! I can't take it anymore, Rob. I never know when either my own mind or somebody else is going to just jolt me into—it's like an earthquake each time, just when I'm least expecting it. I have to have some sort of *preparation.*"

He stares at me steadily, from those blue, blue eyes. Then he whispers, "No."

"No?"

"No. I can't. You told me, Cam—and so did Dr. Newell—that no matter what happened, no matter how many times you changed your mind, I'm not supposed to tell you. It would be worse than not knowing."

"I'll ask Sarah! Joaquim! Mitchell!"

"None of them really knows the true story. Only me and Melita and Mr. C."

"You're lying!" I cry, although I can see that he's not. "Someone else here knows!"

"No one." He's on the edge of tears. But I'm not—I'm furious.

"Fuck it, Rob, it's *my* life!"

"It's your old life. This is the one you have now." He tries to put his arms around me but I fling him off.

"Leave me alone. Now, and for good. I don't want a lover who doesn't care what *I* want or need. Go fuck somebody else." I leave him there, in tears, slamming the door on my way out.

At the far end of the garden, near the Aldani House wall, I throw myself full-length on the bench. Nothing is right anymore. But even when I was afraid of dreams and animals and that soldier girl, I could still dance. I had that. When this interferes with my dancing . . . oh, God, if it makes me so I can't *dance* . . .

If I can't dance, I would rather be dead.

That soldier girl. She knows what happened to me. *I know you had an operation because I saw the result. . . .*

I saw her once in Washington, once in New York. Which city does she live in? I don't even know her name.

A half hour later, it occurs to me that Security at International Center must have her name. They burst into my dressing room and took her off for questioning. And charges were filed; there must be a police report.

It only takes two vid calls. The first, requesting a copy of the police report, puts the report on screen as soon as my ID number verifies that I'm the victim. The girl's name is Shana Irene Walders. No permanent address.

I fret about this for a while, and then I realize that she must have appeared in court—maybe she's in jail someplace that I can visit. Is that allowed? I have no idea. Nor do I know how to find out, so I put in a call to a public database searcher, with rush fees. The PDS calls back almost immediately, and I tell her what I want.

Fifteen minutes later she calls back. "Shana Irene Walders appeared for arraignment in District of Columbia Superior Court on Friday, July 14, 2034, on charges of trespass, criminal intent, and assault of a security officer. Bail was set at $10,000; it was paid by a Dr. Nicholas Clementi. Ms. Walders was released pending a hearing, which was set for Monday, July 31. She gave as 'temporary address' the residence of Dr. Nicholas Clementi, 1396 Sturges Drive, Bethesda, Maryland. Do you wish any more searches?"

"No," I said. "Bill my ID number."

"Thank you for using Sabrina's Search Shop."

Shana Walders, in Bethesda. I have a performance tonight; no, I can't do it. I can't dance the role. Mitchell will have to go on, they can announce that I'm injured, or they can just pretend it's me under Mitchell's mask. . . .My head feels stuffed with something sharp and dangerous, like tacks. If I move the wrong way, they'll pierce my brain and I'll die. Except that if I can't dance, I'm already dead. I can't dance tonight, I would stumble and lurch. . . . I can't go back to the rehearsal. Or the performance. How long will they wait for me? Everyone will just assume I'm late again. And I will be. The late Cameron Atuli, what a shame, so young, a precious natural resource and to kill himself like that at the height of his career. . . .

All that, if I can no longer dance.

I walk to the gate, and through it, and out of Aldani House.

Thirteen ninety-six Sturges Drive in Bethesda is a large, old house. People don't build such large houses anymore, Rob told me; most houses hold only one or two people. Dr. Nicholas Clementi's house has a little lawn in front and

large old trees at the sides and back. From one hangs an ancient wooden swing. The late-afternoon breeze rustles the
leaves, and everything is drenched in golden light like the
Act II curtain of *Sorrows*.

I walk up to the house and ring the bell. A well-dressed
old woman with white hair answers. She says pleasantly,
"Yes?"

"I'd like to see Shana Walders, please."

The woman looks surprised. "May I tell her who's visiting?"

I hesitate, but can't think of any reason not to give my
name. The soldier girl will know me soon enough.
"Cameron Atuli."

The woman's eyes go wide, and she puts her hand to her
mouth. Wordlessly she motions me into a wide center hall.

I would like—would have liked—Rob and me to have a
place like this one day, with sculpture and flowers and
soft pale colors. That's the only thought I have time for
because the soldier girl comes galloping down the stairs.
"Oh my God!"

"Shana Walders?" I say, and my voice comes out high
and squeaky. I try again. "Shana Walders?"

"Where the fuck did *you* come from?"

"I—from Aldani House. I'd like to talk to you."

She laughs, without mirth. "And I been trying to get to
you for . . . but you already know that. Come on." She
grabs my arm. I can't help it; I shrink back.

"Shana," the old woman says, ice in her voice, "what is
happening here?"

"How should I know?" Shana says. "I'm as surprised as
you. Nick isn't home, is he? Well, then, he can hear it all
later. Meanwhile, Mr. Atuli is here to see *me*."

She pulls me into the dining room and shuts the sliding door, leaving the old woman frowning in the hall. The dining room has a polished cherry table, heavy ivory curtains, and eight chairs upholstered in palest green. Beside them, Shana Walders and I look at each other.

"So, Cameron Atuli, what are you doing here?"

I steady myself against a chair back. "I want to know what happened to me. You said in New York that you know." I clasp my hands hard in front of me and wait.

"Why do you want to know now, when you didn't want to know nothing before?" she demands. Clearly she's always demanding. I don't like her.

"None of your business. Just tell me whatever you were going to tell me in New York."

"It would be better if we cooperate." Her voice has changed; she moves close to me and puts her hand on my shoulder, her lips parted a little, her eyes soft and wide. I stare at her incredulously. She moves away and laughs "Just testing. Some of you are bi, right? But not you. All right, then let's swap information."

She talks, then, for a long time. About a train wreck, a warehouse, the chimps she saw with my face, what was said in some government committee. I can hardly bear to hear it. All those dreams of being chased by animals, the cringing at a dog on the street . . . but I don't hear anything that should make me unable to dance. Shana finishes.

I say, "Is that all?"

" 'Is that all?' Don't you care that there are monkeys out there that look like Cameron Atuli, built for women who can't have no kids? No, you don't care. Or not much anyway. But as it happens, that isn't all. Whoever kidnapped you did something else to you."

Suddenly she's uneasy. I wait.

"They cut off your balls," she says brutally. "You are—were—fertile. They probably couldn't get you to come, under torture I mean, and they wanted at least one fertile wad, so they hacked 'em off and took the load of sperm already in there. Fucking bastards." After a minute she says something else, but I can't hear her.

My testicles. They cut them off, because I couldn't come on command. Was there anesthetic? Was I screaming? I can't remember. *You will wonder a thousand thousand times what was in those memories . . .* but not this. Never this. Butchered like meat, still alive but . . . the ghost children of Mr. C.'s new ballet. Children of my body . . . I'd never wanted to father children. But somewhere in my deepest brain, I'd known why I couldn't. Somewhere deeper than memory, somewhere where anger comes from . . . *They cut off my balls.*

Shana Walders is saying, "Hey. Hey, Cameron . . ." and holding out a glass of something. I drink it. Whiskey, burning as it goes down.

I say, "Do you know how hard a blithe man has to work to believe he's a man? In this country, now?"

She stares at me, not understanding. Of course not. She's female, and nobody ever made her doubt she deserved to live. . . . Who made me doubt *myself?* Who made me so afraid? But those memories are closed off forever.

They cut off my balls. . . .

I say, "But I *have* my balls. And I can make love—"

"Synthetic implants. For feel, looks, and hormone-making. But your cum isn't fertile any more. Drink another." Shana holds out more whiskey.

I bat it away and it spills over the pale green carpet.

"Hey—"

"I'll kill them," I say. "I'll kill them all."

Her face brightens. "Well, yeah, *that* makes sense. I mean, they—"

"I'll kill them all. Aldani House has a lawyer. And if he's not good enough, I have money from guest appearances with every major ballet troupe in the world, I'm Cameron Atuli—"

"A *lawyer?* You want to kill them with lawyers? Listen, Atuli, that don't make no sense. The lawyers are on *their* side. The FBI is following you, and Nick Clementi says there's no records of your kidnapping and no police action to find the kidnappers. That means it got blocked at a real high level. The government isn't going to help you, Atuli. They're covering up your torture."

"I don't believe you."

"You believed the rest of it, didn't you?" she demands. "God, you're a stewdee."

I am Cameron Atuli. I am a dancer. I am blithe. I am a dancer. I love Robert Radisson. I am a dancer. And some-one cut off my balls.

I am a dancer.

Anger, I find, is a much stronger partner than fear. Fear stumbles and lurches; anger supports you firmly in what-ever steps you choose.

"Where you going?" Shana says.

I say, "I have a performance in less than two hours. After that . . ." I stop. After that, what? What should come next? I must not lose my anger; I *must not*. My anger is all that's making it possible for me to dance. So after the perfor-mance, what?

Shana says, "You're not going to no performance. You

call up Robert Radisson and tell him to meet us at the Ocean Bar on Georgia Avenue in D.C. It isn't far from Al-dani House."

"Rob? Why?"

"Because I think he's the only person who might know more than us. Even if he don't realize it yet."

"Know what sort of things?" I say.

"Hell, how do I know until I talk to him?" Shana says impatiently. "Just make the call, Atuli."

"I will," I say, and hold onto my anger and feel its power in my legs, my arms, my chest. The power to dance.

I call Rob.

13

NICK CLEMENTI

In Potomac Park, beside the river, stood an "old-fashioned marketplace" trying to look as if it had suddenly sprung up, a commercial Brigadoon, from a hundred years ago. All profits went to support the park, now that the government could no longer afford to do so. The area was kept clean of elderly homeless so tourists could buy pressed-felt fedoras, miniature Model T cars, penny candy, and posters of Franklin Delano Roosevelt and Shirley Temple. The shops were beamed and floored in dark wood; the clerks wore baggy print dresses and garish lipstick. *Safe in the hallowed quiets of the Past . . .* Right.

The public "phone booths" were small individual sheds, each with a wooden seat, glassed in for privacy. None had vid. They took coins. I eased myself onto a seat, closed the door, and gazed at the "Instructions For Dialing," which you had to do to reach a link. But the link itself was real enough. A secretary program answered my call. "Good afternoon. Tymbal, Kramer, and Anderson."

"Joshua Tymbal, please."

"I'm sorry, Mr. Tymbal is in a—"

"Tell him it's Nick Clementi calling, and it's urgent."

"Just a moment . . ." and then, "Nick! How long has it been?"

"Years. I keep up with you, though, through the Harvard Online Class Notes. It all sounds good, Josh."

"You haven't done so bad yourself. But my program said it was urgent. . . ." He hadn't changed since Harvard. Still impatient, just this side of rude, willing to cut social corners to get things his way. Which was why I was calling him now.

"Josh, it is urgent. But it's also a shot in the dark. My son is married now—"

"Congratulations!" he boomed, as if this were news. John and Laurie have been married for three years, and Josh attended the wedding, which was full of important people he wanted to meet.

"Thanks. Only they've been trying hard to conceive, and . . . Well, you know how it is. So we're looking into adoption. They know—I know—how hard it is to even find a baby, and how many applicants there are for each one. I know that adoption is part of your legal practice. . . ."

"Was," he said heavily. "Not much business there nowadays."

"I know. But the family really wants this, and we're willing to throw all our resources, which are considerable by now, behind the effort . . . *all* our resources. . . ."

He understood. I knew it from his silence. But I had misjudged him—and why not? All I had to go on were old memories, a few meetings spread over fifty years, and reading between the carefully neutral lines of the Harvard alumni bulletins.

"Nick . . . I think you have the wrong attorney. I haven't been able to arrange adoptions, of any kind, for years now."

All very correct. He didn't know my call was untraceable. And I didn't know who had access to his records. I said, "I'm sorry to hear that, Josh. It was just a hope. I'm trying every avenue I can, of course."

"Of course." But then he said, "You might try Ted Panzardi. Do you remember him? Big guy, played hockey. He was All-Ivy one year."

"No. Is he is Washington?"

"Baltimore, I think. I haven't actually heard from him in years. But someone casually mentioned to me that he arranges . . . adoptions."

In the stuffy "phone booth," I grinned. Tymbal was covering his ass. I hadn't completely misremembered him after all; he might not do black-market adoptions himself, but he was in the loop.

"Thanks, Josh," I said. "I owe you one."

"Of course," he said lightly, but it wasn't light. It was the whole point.

Ted Panzardi was cautious. But he knew who I was, and he talked to me long enough to set up a meeting at a public restaurant.

I went on down my list, which was long. Scientific colleagues I'd always suspected of less-than-perfect ethics. Harvard alumni. People I'd met over the years in Washington. I had never done this before, but it turned out the wall between legitimate business and the black market, even in something as precious as human life, was thin, and riddled with passageways. Probably the lawyers and doctors didn't think they were doing anything wrong. The babies, after all, ended up in affluent homes that desperately wanted them. The lawyers ended up well compensated. And the biological mothers . . . well, was a girl who was willing to conceive and sell a child fit to be a mother? I set up two more meetings on neutral turf, no promises, "Let's just discuss your needs."

But under the self-protective, self-satisfied greed, I heard another note. An odd regret. Not the regret of morality, but the regret of a supplier without enough product to meet market demand.

No one else wanted to use the "phone booth"—in fact, no one else seemed to be visiting the tourist village. At this rate, the place would never yield park revenues. The old didn't want to be reminded of the past, and the young knew too strongly that they were the future. We'd told them so often enough. *Let the dead bury the dead. . . .*

My eye hurt, the sore in my mouth was worse, and the headache was back.

But I'd almost worked my way through my list of names. Next: Billy McCullough, whom I remembered as a scholarship kid from North Philadelphia that I'd felt constrained to be decent to because my classmates were not. Billy had flunked out our sophomore year. Still, with pathetic pride, he still sent in his yearly reports to the Class Notes, and they still posted them. He had finished college elsewhere, gone to a third-rate law school, opened a practice back in Philadelphia. I didn't know that city well enough to tell if the address was a decent one. I hoped not.

"Billy McCullough? This is Nick Clementi. We were at Harvard together. You probably don't remember me—"

"Yes, I do," he said. "How are you, Nick?"

"Old. Like all of us. But I'm calling for a specific reason, Billy. I was hoping you could help me. . . ." I went through the whole spiel. My head pounded. Very soon I would have to take medication, lie down in a cab.

"Yeah," Billy McCullough said finally. "I can hear what you want. I can help you."

"You can?" His tone was definite, almost angry.

"Yeah. Listen, I'm in a new office. Brand new; I just rented it this morning. Nobody knew I was going to, so nothing's tapped or monitored. What about you? A public phone, right?"

He knew the subroutines. I sat up straighter. "Right."

"Okay. I'm going to talk straight to you. You were always straight to me, and I know you're sincere about what you want. You want a black market baby for your son. But I'm telling you, there aren't any. Five years ago, even three . . . just maybe. But not now. Not enough of the girls we use here and abroad are getting pregnant, and it's harder all the time to find new ones, at any price. You understand?"

"Yes, I said. *The girls we use here and abroad.* What was I becoming a part of?

"Okay. But a lot of women want babies. So sometimes we offer substitutes. They sound surprising at first, but take my word for it, women come to really love them. Sometimes they hardly know the difference, after a while. And a bonus: they're a lot less expensive than a newborn. You interested?"

I said slowly, "I don't know. What exactly are we talking about, Billy?"

"Okay, I'll tell you. But you got to reserve judgment when you first hear. You got to keep an open mind. That shouldn't be hard for you, you're a scientist. And you got to trust that I've done this before, I've seen how women react after the first shock, how they get to love their little substitutes. And why not—they look like toddlers, they walk like toddlers, they hold up their adorable little hands to be picked up, they respond to love. And they look completely human. You can believe me on this, Nick—dressed, they look completely human. With the intelligence of a year-old human baby. They color with crayons, they play with toys, you can feed 'em a bottle."

"And what are they in actuality?" It was difficult to get the words out.

"Human. At least, human faces and hands. Completely, created by vivifacture."

"And put on . . . what?"

"Purebred intelligent baby chimps. That, once they're dressed in little human clothes and shoes, your daughter-in-law won't be able to tell from any other baby. And after she spends time cuddling and feeding her little one, she won't care. Believe me; I've seen it time and time again."

Time and time again. "You place a lot of these substitutes, Billy?"

"You wouldn't believe how many. Or who some of the families are who adopt them. I can't name names, of course—but your son will be in some very tony company. And the little one can even look like him. We have a selection. You were blond, I remember, Nick, northern Italian—is your son blond too? We have an adorable little girl, looks like a Sáxon princess. And smart as Einstein."

"No . . . I . . . give me a minute, Billy. This is all so new."

"Course it is," Billy said amiably. "But you're making all the right moves. I have your call traced, of course. FDR

Village is good. Probably thousands of tourists through there every day, right?"

I rested my head back against the cool glass. My headache made it difficult to think. How much longer before the coma?

"Nick? You there?"

"Yes. Billy, I don't want blond. If we're really going to do this . . . Laurie, my daughter-in-law, has a mixed background. Some French, some Hispanic, some black. It might help persuade her if you—if we—could show her a . . . a little one with something like her looks." He hadn't been invited to Laurie's wedding; he wouldn't know what she looked like.

"Okay," he said eagerly. "Describe her."

"It's an unusual face. Dark hair, light brown skin, hazel eyes flecked with gold, full lips . . . she looks like she could be anything. People never guess her background. Last Halloween, she even put on a red wig and was convincing as an Irish leprechaun."

"Okay, Nick, I'll phone around. There's a supply network, of course. Let's set up a meeting for a few days from now, and maybe I'll even have holos to show you. I'll come to Washington."

We chose a place and time. No money was mentioned; that would come later. Billy could have been a successful legitimate salesman, if, even over vidless phone, he weren't so repulsive.

I took my meds, phoned for a cab, and tried to think. I could have the cops with me at the meeting—but an FBI agent had talked a long time to Cameron Atuli, and Van Grant had lied to me about Atuli's kidnapping. I didn't know how far this coverup (of what?) extended, or why, or who was safe to confide in. So perhaps no cops. Not yet.

I thought of bringing home to Laurie a chimp with Cameron Atuli's face on it, and I shuddered. What was I doing? I'd planned only on buying a baby for Laurie, not on all this. . . . Everything looked different from this angle, so different from when I'd seen the artist's drawing of Shana Walders's chimps on the antiseptic wall screen of the Congressional Advisory Committee for Medical Crises.

Shana. Was she home yet from wherever she'd gone?

I struggled out of the cab and up the sidewalk. The trees and grass around me kept wavering, swooping. It was better if I closed my right eye. But something was happening in my brain. . . .

I leaned on the bell. Inside my house raucous music blared, which meant Shana *was* home. But she didn't open the door, nor did Maggie. It was Sallie, standing there with her hair wild, saying in a bitter voice, "I've been fired. After fifteen years. They found my intrusion into the Atuli file— Dad? What's wrong?"

"Call . . . your mother."

"Dad! What is it! Mom!"

The room went dark. I was conscious, but I couldn't see. The mucor fibers had finally reached the optic canal. Strangely enough, the vertigo suddenly passed, and I felt a weird calm. But I didn't know this new territory. I stepped forward and stumbled, and it was Maggie who caught me in her arms and led me, blind, to a chair I could feel but no longer see.

As deaths go, mucormycosis occupies a middle ground. Not as painful and prolonged as some of the vanquished cancers, not as swift and merciful as some cardiac events. I would have seizures, then a coma which would be far worse for Maggie than for me, who would know nothing of it.

But for the moment, sitting in my hospital bed, I was only weak. Not in pain. My doctors had come and gone with their meds and scans and calibrations, which all of us knew made no difference whatsoever. I had, forcefully for my present condition, insisted that Maggie and Sallie go home to sleep. Reluctantly, to please me, they had.

I could see. Only dimly, but from both eyes. That told me that the primary lesion was either at the optic chiasma or along the optic radiation. If it had been less far into my skull, at the retinal end of the optic nerve, I would still have intact vision in one eye. If it had been in the visual cortex, I'd have remained totally blind.

As it was, the foot of my hospital bed was a metal blur. The curtains across the room looked like fuzzy patches. Something sat on the windowsill—flowers? water carafe?— but not even squinting told me what it was.

Sound was suddenly more solid than sight. Beyond my window traffic hummed, even at this hour, the soothing subdued monotony of a remote waterfall. In the unseen hallway, footsteps stopped by my door, paused, padded on. I lay quietly, hearing them go.

Neither the sun nor death can be looked at steadily. La Rochefoucauld.

But I had tried. I had pushed away from myself the despairs, entreaties, angers of someone who cannot bear the thought of his individual mind gone from the universe. Not for me undignified fury against the inevitable. I would be different. Serene, accepting. Unafraid. And, in my own judgment, I had been.

What I hadn't realized, until now, was that it wasn't fear that made dying so difficult. Nor fury. It wasn't the fight to hold onto the tide that would, must, obey the dictates of the physical world and ebb forever. It wasn't rage that a lifetime of self would just cease to exist, like a snuffed candle. The metaphors were all wrong, and far too grand.

It was much more like having to leave a meeting before the whole agenda had been worked through.

I could part with my life. I could even leave Maggie, whose own life, comparatively speaking, did not have that much longer to run without me. But how could I leave Laurie in the middle of her mind-cracking hunger for a child? How could I leave John before he'd finished growing up? How could I leave Sallie, newly fired from the CDC because of me? How could I even leave that little wretch Shana, dangerous to herself and everybody else, as she mucked around with forces orders of magnitude more powerful than she? How could I leave in the middle of the story, before I found out how it all came out?

The middle of the story. Yes, it had begun to feel like that, a story in which only part of me participated, the rest already closing the pages, already elsewhere. But I still wanted the story to come out right.

O death all eloquent, you only prove/What dust we dote on, when 'tis man we love. Pope.

Just once, I'd like to have thought of something that hadn't already been said infinitely better by the dead.

Slowly I shifted against my pillow. Somewhere down the dim hall, someone moaned. Someone else, or perhaps just a nursing program, murmured softly. All this—strange thought, still, despite everything—would continue after I did not. But until that moment actually came, I had to think how to address the items left on the agenda, and help the people who could not go with me when I escaped the rest of the meeting.

14

SHANA WALDERS

I can't believe it. I blow weeks and money and a semi-good police record trying to get to Cameron Atuli, and then he walks into Nick's house. Just walks in. Go figure.

We're alone in the dining room a long time. I turn on a music chip, real loud, so nobody can't hear us talk. When we come out, Maggie's already gone, which explains why Her Highness didn't hammer on the dining room door while I grilled Atuli. Sallie, who's up from Atlanta in a bloodboil about something, isn't home neither. The front door even stands halfway open, like they left the house in a big hurry. That isn't like neither of them. But I don't have no time to think about this.

"You sure he'll be waiting there?" I ask Atuli.

"He'll be there," he says, his handsome jaw set. It's clear he don't want to talk much, so I shut up during the train ride to D.C. Atuli's a weird program—one minute he's all quivery and upset, the next grim and angry. And he lets all of it show, which is just stupid. You have to shield yourself.

I lead us on and off trains until I'm sure nobody isn't following us. The Ocean Bar, in D.C., is a toilet pit trying to look like an aquarium. Holo mermaids swim through the air, and the table menus are shaped like shells. But at this hour the bar is empty—at least, in the public room—and the order program don't keep pestering you about how long you sit without ordering more drinks. Radisson waits at a back table, looking even more quivery than Atuli. His voice is soft and tender.

"Cameron?"

"I'm sorry I yelled at you, Rob. So sorry." Atuli reaches for his hand, and Radisson grabs on like he's drowning. It's like I don't exist.

"Okay, break it up," I say, sitting down. "Not here, for fuck's sake. Radisson, we got some questions for you, and they're important."

Radisson looks at Atuli, who says, "This is Shana Walders. Yes, she's the same one. She told me some things, Rob, about . . . before my operation. Things you already know, and some you don't. Will you help us?"

"Help you do what?" Radisson says, and I see he don't like this. But Atuli's on fire again, angry and hard, and Radisson don't want to risk another spat now that he just got Atuli back. Rucky-fuckies.

"Help him find out who mangled his nuts," I say. *I'm going to be in charge here.* "Tell us everything you can remember."

Radisson hesitates and Atuli, his voice splintery, says, "Please."

"Last January nineteenth," Radisson says in a low voice, "you left Aldani House to go shopping. You wouldn't let me come with you because you were buying an anniversary present for me. And you just . . . disappeared."

"Did Aldani House call the cops?" I ask.

"Not right away. They won't come, you know, for a missing adult, only for missing kids. And Mr. C. knew that you and I had had a . . . a quarrel."

"Mr. C. knew that?" Atuli says, and I don't get the anguish in his voice.

"Who's Mr. C.?"

They both look at me like I turned purple. "Mr. *Col-lelouri*," Radisson finally says. "The *choreographer.*"

Like I'm supposed to know what one is. But I just nod and Radisson goes on.

"Before we ever did call the cops, the FBI showed up. They said they'd found you in a raid on an illegal vivifac-ture lab in Baltimore. You were . . . badly hurt. Mr. C. and Melita went to the hospital, and I threw a fit until they took me, too."

"What hospital?" I say.

"Carter Memorial. There was a federal marshall guard-ing your room. People kept coming and going, FBI and doctors and such. They wouldn't let me see you. They said you were hysterical, almost psychotic. Finally, three days later, Melita took me aside and said they were going to do an induced retrograde amnesia, that you were going psy-chotic without it and it was either that or keep you so heav-ily drugged you'd never be able to dance again."

I say, "So they wiped his memory so they didn't lose a good moneymaking dancer," and again they both look at me like I'm a dead fish.

Atuli says, "The alternative was *not to dance.*"

"So? You could do something else."

Atuli shakes his head. He's holding Radisson's hand again; good thing this dump is empty. "The same thing hap-pened when we started a ballet about fertility . . . at some level, my brain knew. Even when *I* didn't know. It's all tied together, somehow: dancing and . . . what they did to me. . . . Go on, Rob."

But I say, "Who signed? For the operation. If he was psycho, a family member would of had to sign."

Atuli's hand tightens on his lover's. I suddenly see that this is where he learns if he's got any family. But Radisson says to me, "Mr. C. signed. Cameron only has an uncle and cousins, all of who threw him out long ago, for . . . for loving men. So Mr. C. signed."

They don't see nothing wrong with this, apparently, but I know better. Atuli wasn't no minor, and this Mr. C. had no right. Somebody was bending rules all over the place.

"I knew what an induced amnesia would mean," Radisson says, his voice husky now. "You wouldn't even remember me, Cam. Not anything that we'd been to each other. I couldn't bear it. I had to see you once more, no matter what. So in the middle of the night I bribed the marshall—"

"With what?" I say, interested.

Radisson suddenly blushes bright red. So that works for rucky-fuckies, too! But then Radisson says, "With all the money I had saved," and I see that the blush was for this supposed crime of bribery. Dancers are weird.

I say, "So you got in to see Atuli in the middle of the night. This is the important part, Radisson. Tell us everything he said. Everything." A horrible thought hits me. "Was Atuli raving crazy?"

"No. He was . . . they'd given you some drug, Cam, to calm you down. You were crying, but slowly, heavily, like nothing mattered any more. That was the drugs. But you recognized me, and we talked, and I . . . made love to you. I thought it might be the last time ever. They said that after the operation, I couldn't ever tell you how we'd been together . . . or anything else about the past. I had to let you move on. So I got into that narrow little bed with you, and—"

"No pervert stuff," I say. "Just tell us what Atuli *said* to you."

Radisson don't even look at me. His gaze is glued to Atuli. "You said three men had grabbed you and forced you into a car. You described how they took tissue samples and MOSS readings and then they brought in a porn holo for you to . . . give a semen sample. But you wouldn't—"

No wonder, I think—probably the porn was of a girl. But I don't say it out loud.

"—so one of the men said, 'Then just take the whole thing, and we'll test it that way. We're going to delete him anyway.' And . . . they did."

He stops. I'm going to want a lot more details than this, but not just yet. I say, "Radisson, did they say anything— anything that Atuli repeated to you, anyway—to show that they knew he was a world-famous dancer?"

"No," Radisson says.

"Did Atuli say anything about the location of this place, or the place Atuli's balls and tissue samples were going to, or the men's names, or anything?"

"Yes," Radisson says, and I draw in a breath. Atuli's face is still stone.

Radisson says, this time to me, "Cam told me that he was in the car for exactly fifty-five minutes. They didn't take his wrister away, and he timed it. They didn't blindfold him. When he got out, it was in a parking lot all overgrown with weeds. He glimpsed the outside of the building across the street—it was boarded-up old-style concrete blocks, with a name in faded paint. KANG, LTD. He could smell the ocean, and there were seagulls overhead. The men called each other 'Zuger,' 'Meyerhoff,' and 'Doctor.' He described them for me. They argued in front of him about which of two places to send the tissues, and they decided on 'Emily Jogerst,' in Philadelphia, because she had the best contacts even though she didn't pay the highest price."

"Jesus" is all I can think of to say. Here it is. The bastards weren't careful at all; they'd expected to kill Atuli, so it didn't matter what he heard. We got actual names and places.

Which means so does the FBI. But a case like this—Atuli's face on chimps—would have been all over the newsgrids as soon as charges were filed. Which means either no charges are filed yet while the feds follow through, or that they're sitting on the whole thing. Which?

I say to Radisson, "Who else did you tell any of this to?"

"No one."

"Not the feds?"

"They didn't find out I'd been in to see Cam. And when they asked what else, if anything, I knew, I said nothing. They'd have had it all from Cam anyway, wouldn't they, with truth drugs?"

"Yeah. They would." I don't know what the feds are doing with their information. But whatever it is, it won't magically clear me of lying in front of Congress so I can get into the army. Nobody isn't going to bother with that little detail, unless I do it myself. And now I have a name. Emily Jogerst. In Philadelphia.

Where in Philadelphia?

A human being finally appears in the doorway at the back of the bar. He notices Atuli and Radisson holding hands across the table, and he scowls hard. I get them out of there, and I walk between them while we find someplace else to talk. I need more information, all the information Radisson has, before I can plan what to do next.

Maggie, who's still not home, is the same size as me, just a little smaller in the tits and thicker in the waist. I stand in her bedroom trying on clothes I could never afford, and wouldn't buy if I could. Calf-length dresses, loose flowing vests. Old-lady stuff, without no flash. "How about this red one?" I say to Atuli, who sits in a bedroom chair, watching me.

"I still don't like the whole idea," he says, scowling.

"You got a better one? No. What about the dress?"

"Too tight in the bust," Atuli says. "You're trying to look rich, for God's sake. And that color isn't right for you. Put the blue one back on."

"I fade out in the blue one!"

"You're supposed to fade out. You're a young rich matron, not a hooker."

I yank the red dress over my head and stand fuming in my underwear. Atuli don't react, of course. I pull the blue dress back on, pale silk, cut soft and full, hardly don't show my figure at all. And it goes down past my knees. With a stewdee ruffle of cream-colored lace on the attached vest. Atuli nods. "Yes. In that one you look believable. Sort of."

He gets up and gathers my hair into a low knot at the back of my head, like the ballerinas wear. The front he slicks smooth with pomade, and then tips his head to eye me critically. "Yes. But I'm going to do your makeup. Wash your face."

I let him, hating what he does. Maggie's pale old-lady colors, and hardly none of those. But I have to admit that when he's done, I look like what I'm supposed to be: a rich boring girl who could be Laurie Clementi. I'm even blonde like her, although the difference is buttercups to baby shit.

"Yes," Atuli says. "Now let's go, before anyone comes home."

"You're not going with me!" I yell, for maybe the millionth time. "They *know* you, stewdee. They cut off your balls, remember? One sight of you and it's over. You can't go."

"I can go as far as the Philadelphia train station."

"No. I don't want you cluttering up my movements. Go back to Aldani House, Atuli, like I told you."

He says, "And suppose you need physical help?"

I laugh. "From you? A rucky-fucky dancer?"

His face darkens and he moves away from me. Suddenly, in a blur, I'm on the floor, pinned. I try all my tricks, but he don't let go. He's strong, and fast, and *trained*. I pant, "Where'd you learn that?"

"I don't know. But dance is an athletic discipline, asshole."

I struggle some more, but he's really good. Finally I thrust my face up suddenly and kiss him full on the lips. He lets me go like I'm poison ivy, and I laugh. "Too bad, Atuli. You don't know what you're missing. But you're still not going with me."

He glares at me. All of a sudden I see that he needs to stay angry, that the anger is fueling him. It's the first thing about him I've understood.

"Listen," I say. "Don't worry about me. And there's something I need you to do here. If I don't call you at Aldani House by twenty-four hours from now, then you have to come back here and tell the whole story to Nick. He can get high-level cops involved if he has to—he told me so. Tell him everything. But only if you don't hear nothing from me, okay?"

"Yes," he says, but will he do it? Guys like him usually just run away from scary situations.

Before we leave the house, I write a note to Nick and Maggie: *Not home tonite. Hot date with gorjus guy.* They'll believe that, all right, or at least Maggie will. She thinks I'm a slut. Too bad she can't see me in her boring blue dress.

Two blocks down the street, Atuli snaps, "For God's sake, don't walk like that. You're supposed to look like a young wife, not a hooker."

"I know what I'm supposed to look like and I know how to do it when the time comes! Leave me the fuck alone!"

We glare at each other, and then he says suddenly, surprising me, "Shana. Be careful."

"Don't worry about me. I can take care of myself. I'll phone you."

He nods and starts off in the opposite direction. He really does have a cute butt. What a waste.

I walk carefully to the nearest station and catch a train to Philadelphia.

It's not so hard to find people as you might think, even in a big strange city. Not if you know the kind of people you're looking for, and have someplace to start.

People running large-scale underground markets need large-scale aboveground fronts. It accounts for the trucks and visitors and stuff, and it gives the local cops someplace to say they didn't know was illegal if their payoffs get investigated. At South Station I simply use the public vid directory. There are two "E. Jogerst's."

I call the first one. An old man comes on-line. "May I speak to Emily Jogerst?"

"No Emily here, just me," he growls, and blanks. Okay. Try the other code.

"May I speak to Emily Jogerst?"

"May I ask what this is in reference to?" the pleasant middle-aged holo in a business vest says. Behind her—it— is an office that might of been any office anyplace, or just another holo.

I make my voice soft and scared. "It's . . . personal. Mr. Meyerhoff sent me."

"Just a moment."

Long delay. They're tracing. I smooth my hand over my hair to make sure it's still stuffed into the stewdee ballerina bun. People hurry past in South Station, under a high ceiling so gritty it must not of been cleaned in fifty years. Or maybe it was built like that.

"Hello. This is Emily Jogerst. You've reached Martin Medical Supplies, Inc. Was that what you wanted?"

Meyerhoff must usually use a different number. Be careful. I look confused and even more scared. "I . . . don't know. I lost the number Mr. Meyerhoff gave me, so I just looked in the directory. . . . I'm Laurie Clementi. I'm looking for . . . a job." And I hold my breath. If there's supposed to be a code word, I've blown it. "Job" is the best I could come up with, after a lot of thought on the train. It could mean employment, or delivery, or . . .

"I see. May I have your citizen ID number, Ms. Clementi?"

I give her Laurie's number. It's amazing what people leave around in their files when they got house guests. Old tax returns, family records, vid pictures, notes to themselves.

"Where can I reach you in a few minutes? Naturally we

do a background check before we offer employment inter-
views, even with recommendations."

Jesus, does she think Meyerhoff really recommended
me for employment? I stammer, "Well, right now I'm at the
train station, I'm from out of town. . . ."

"Please give me that number."

I do, and she blanks. I spend ten minutes fidgeting on a
bench, watching all the old people hobbling past. Two
moldy ladies together, cackling and laughing like kids.
What have *they* got to laugh about? An old fart with a
walker, inching his way along. Then another one. Not even
the one or two young men hit on me. Looking like a young
matron is boring.

The vid rings and I jump for it. "Your employment cre-
dentials check out, Ms. Clementi, and as it happens we
need another secretary immediately. Could you possibly
meet me for dinner?"

I burble all pretty, "Oh, yes, of course, thank you,
where?"

She gives me an address and a time, and after an hour of
wasting time in a VR parlor programmed like the Mars
colonies, I get a cab. The restaurant is small, one of those
places where there's only three things every day on the
menu and the chef cooks them all himself fresh. I walk in
like Laurie Clementi, who I met at a family dinner at Dr.
Clementi's house, and who everybody treats like she's
some sort of precious gift made out of breakable glass.

"Ms. Clementi? Here."

Emily Jogerst is maybe fifty, big-boned but pretty,
dressed in clothes like mine. Like Maggie's. Her eyes are
lasers. I smile shyly and drop my napkin and bite my lip
and otherwise look bothered and nervous. We chitchat

about the menu, we order drinks. I ask for a wine that Nick once served at his house.

"Now, let's talk," Jogerst says pleasantly. "You're Mrs. John Clementi, and you need a . . . job."

At dinner Laurie looked so honest you wanted to kick her. I say, "Ms. Jogerst, what I need is . . . I can't have a baby. And we've tried so hard."

If this really *is* a job interview, that should make Jogerst think I'm nuts. But she says, "You've visited three different fertility clinics, over three years."

Did I? I don't know *that* much about Laurie Clementi. But I nod.

"You and your husband are not wealthy people," Jogerst says.

I rush in with, "No, but my husband is—"

"—Dr. Nicholas Clementi's son. Who stands to inherit quite a bit. But not just yet, and of course there are other heirs."

"Oh, but my father-in-law will help us now! He wants a grandchild just as much as John and I want a baby!"

Jogerst nods. "Yes, we know that." *How*, for fucking sake? She adds, "Does he know you're here now?"

"No." I look down at the table. "I wanted to . . . to investigate the situation first."

"And how do you know Mr. Meyerhoff?" She's looking at me real sharp.

I take a deep breath. This is my weak link. "I'm sorry, but I can't tell you that. The person who gave me the name asked me not to. She's an old friend."

"Someone we've helped previously?"

I say nothing, though that's exactly what I want her to think. These rich people must have their own underground word-of-mouth. Somewhere Laurie Clementi must know somebody who's done fertility on the black market, even if Laurie don't know she knows.

"I see," Jogerst says. "Well, then, let's proceed to what you've heard about what we can do for you. You know we don't deal in newborn babies?"

"I know. And I . . . we . . . couldn't afford that anyway. But I know someone who has . . . I think I could love a substitute baby."

"A pet?"

"If it looked human. Like . . . a chimpanzee with a human face. I could love it."

There—I laid down my cards. She says, "And how do you know we can provide such a thing?"

"The same way I heard about you."

Jogerst goes on studying me. I see the moment she comes to a decision. "I see. Mrs. Clementi, there is sometimes a gap between what we visualize and what is actually offered. Before you and I talk any further, I'd like you to see one of our little ones. If you don't mind delaying your meal a few minutes, I can show you an adorable little one now."

"Here?"

She smiles. "In the parking lot, of course. In my van."

I look eager, which isn't hard because I am. They exist. They're real. And if I can bring one to Nick and he can take it to that fucking Congressional committee to prove I wasn't lying. . . . US Army, here I come. Weapons training. Maybe someday be a non-com. . . .

Jogerst says something to the maitre d' and leads me out a back door. Her van, with heavily opaqued windows, is parked so the back opens into a corner made by two high fences. We squeeze behind the van and she unlocks it. I suddenly wonder if this particular chimp will have Atuli's face. But that would be too much of a coincidence, an operation this slick must have a choice of chimp babies—

A man leans out of the back of the open van and grabs me.

I don't even have time to scream. His hand clamps my mouth shut, followed immediately by tape. He snaps on manacles, wrists and ankles. Jogerst climbs in behind me and slams the door. The unseen driver starts us moving.

"Now, we'll talk," Jogerst says to me. "One way or another." I try to kick her, but the manacles are fastened to the side of the van and the chain don't reach that far. She laughs and studies me.

"You're pretty good, I'll give you that. Laurie Clementi's ID number, medical history, life story. If it hadn't been for Billy McCullough, I might have bought the whole thing."

Billy McCullough? Who's that? I duck away from the man taking my retina scan. He tries again and gets it, jamming the scanner against my eye so hard that I'll have a shiner.

Jogerst says, "I see you don't know that Dr. Clementi already contacted us through McCullough about a little one for Laurie. And he described Laurie Clementi: 'mixed background, some French, some Hispanic, some black. Dark hair, light brown skin, hazel eyes flecked with gold.' . . . That's certainly not *you*."

And not fucking Laurie either! But I can't say this through the tape on my mouth. The retina man looks up from a portable terminal, puzzled. "Em. She's not a cop."

Jogerst frowns. "What do you mean, not a cop?"

"She's not on file in our law deebee."

"Then send the scan to Duffy and tell him to look through NCIS! See if she's there!"

"Okay." He goes back to his terminal and murmurs to it. Jogerst turns her back on me. I sit manacled and try to think, but I'm too scared. They did a retina scan when they arrested me for assaulting Atuli at the International Center. I'm on file. If Jogerst has dirty access to NCIS, she'll find out who I am. They'd of killed me even if I was a cop—she wouldn't have mentioned McCullough in front of me otherwise—but I'm not a cop. I'm a homeless nobody.

A beautiful homeless nobody. With a gorgeous baby-firm face.

They done this before. That's why the restaurant looks the other way when Jogerst and guest disappear into the parking lot and don't return for dinner. That's why there's a choice of human faces on a baby chimp. . . .

How long will it take? How much will it hurt? And what will they do to find out if *I'm* fertile and have eggs to harvest?

You're pretty good, I'll give you that. If it hadn't been for Billy McCullough, I might have bought the whole thing.

But not good enough. Only gorgeous enough. Only that.

15

NICK CLEMENTI

"Maggie," I said, "I'm feeling much better. I'd like to see Shana, if I may."

Her hand tightened on mine. I could see her, although not clearly. My vision was permanently dimmed—whatever "permanently" meant in this context. Maggie's face was a pale blur against the high back of the hospital "visitor chair," which in some misguided attempt at cheer was a vivid yellow, even to me.

"Shana didn't come home last night, Nick. She left a note that she had a date." Despite the strain—we both knew I would probably never leave this hospital room—Maggie's voice remained steady. She had always been brave. John and Laurie and Sallie had all been various degrees of hysterical, but not Maggie.

"Maggie. There's something I need you to do, sweetheart."

"For Shana?"

"Partly. But mostly for me."

The blur that was my wife shifted slightly. "Go on."

"I've been trying to help Laurie. She . . . you see how she is."

"Yes. She's become . . . go on, Nick. What have you done?"

"Tried to find her a baby on the black market."

Maggie was silent, absorbing this. "I thought you were going to tell me when you began work on that. Why didn't you let me help?"

"There wasn't anything for you to do. Not yet, not then. But something . . . happened."

Now her voice sharpened. "What happened? Does it involve that wretched Shana?"

"I'm afraid so. But it involves more than her. Listen carefully, sweetheart. There's a lawyer named Billy McCullough, a man I was at Harvard with. I called him to find out if he could arrange something for Laurie. And instead of an infant, which he said was not to be had at any price, although I'm not sure I believe him about that—instead of an infant, he offered me a chance to—"

"Dr. Clementi," the room system said, "you have a visitor."

Maggie said irritably, "Dr. Clementi asked not to be disturbed."

"Yes, ma'am," the program answered. "But the visitor overrode your preference. He said—"

"I said it was a matter of life and death," the visitor said from the doorway. "Maggie, how are you?"

"Good Lord," she said wonderingly. "I'm surprised to see—what do you mean, a matter of life and death? Nick, it's Vanderbilt Grant."

She didn't have to tell me. I knew it was Van, not only from his voice but from the atmosphere in the room. He filled it even when I could barely see him: a solar presence, everyone else turning toward him with inevitable biological tropism.

"Hello, Nick," he boomed. "I've got good news. And I wanted to tell you myself." The Commissioner of the Food and Drug Administration strode toward the opposite side of the bed from Maggie. A part of my mind noted that he didn't move, and didn't talk, like a man approaching someone dying. He took my other hand.

"Nick, listen. We had a new report come in yesterday. Now, you know that the FDA can't possibly keep up with all the drug review work with my present staff. Just impossible. So we farm out a lot of the initial investigations to private labs. After the drug company files an official New Drug Application, of course, we're right on top of it ourselves. And even before that, we keep tabs on the preliminary investigations."

Van paused. I was tempted to think the pause was for effect, but there was something about his posture as he leaned over my bed. . . . My heart started a slow, rhythmic thumping.

"The private companies that do investigative work for us also do backup testing for a lot of overseas companies. So sometimes they hear of a foreign development before any of us. And that's just happened. LeGrand-Wu, in Paris, just requested Stage Three testing for a new drug. It's DNA-based, of course, France doesn't have the same restrictions we do on germ-line manipulation. The drug affects the ability of certain fungal cells to reproduce. One of the fungi it has been effective is stopping is mucormycosis."

"Oh, my God," Maggie said. Her hand tightened so hard on mine that her ring cut into my fingers.

"In clinical trials, *one hundred percent effective*," Van went on triumphantly. "But there's no time to lose. I could arrange a Compassionate Use Import Exception for you, Nick, through the State Department. But believe it or not, it's actually faster to send you to the drug rather than go through channels to get the drug to you. And then you'll be where there are people experienced with the followup procedures."

Maggie said. "In *France?* But look at him, Van, he can't travel—"

"Yes, he can. I've taken the liberty of arranging a medical helicopter to take him to Dulles. And a military flight from there. The copter should be here in a few minutes. You go, too, Maggie, of course. In Paris the—"

"*Wait,*" I said.

I could feel them both looking at me.

"You mean . . . you mean . . ." and then, to my own horror, I could feel my throat close and the tears spill over the thin sensitive skin under my eyes.

I was not going to die.

"Oh, Nick, don't . . . I mean, do, go ahead, it's so wonderful!" Maggie cried. And Van beamed—I could feel it, even through my semi-blindness, even through my tears— he beamed like a man who just saved the world. Which, in a sense, he had.

I was not going to die.

"Wait," I said, so thickly that this time nobody understood me, including me. Wait? For what? I was being handed a reprieve, a second chance. . . . Outside the window, I heard the drone of a helicopter. "Wait . . ."

"Can't wait," Van boomed cheerfully. "Got to save your life, boy. God, there's some days I like my job. Of course, you know we can't regenerate nerves, you're not going to regain your sight, but that and all other damage can be halted right here, right now, right in its tracks!"

He was like a kid, triumphant over winning a softball

game, practically jumping up and down. And Maggie was crying and hugging me. Medics came in with a stretcher and began to transfer me to it from the bed, mouthing the mundane directions they'd given a thousand times before, "Now, just relax, sir, we're going to lift you, it'll only take a minute, here we go. . . ." And all the while my mind had gone numb, unable to take it in.

I was not going to die.

But I was *prepared* to die.

"Careful carrying him," Maggie said, "mind that door jamb there. . . ."

What I was not prepared to do was go on living.

"I'll be in close and constant touch," Van said somewhere behind me as I was carried swiftly down the corridor and into an elevator. The elevator door closed.

"The chopper's on the roof, sir," a medic said. "We're just going to go up to the roof and then outside for a few minutes. It'll be very windy. Be prepared for that."

Be prepared. . . . I go to prepare you a place. . . . Prepare to fire. . . . "Maggie," I said blindly, "Maggie . . ."

"I'm here, love. I'm here."

"Here we go, sir, just a quick lift into the chopper . . . Ed, secure him. . . ."

"Maggie . . . why now? Why this lifesaver right now?"

She said radiantly, "Because sometimes *somebody* has to win, love. Sometimes the universe comes through."

But that wasn't what I'd meant.

Much of the trip was vague. I think the medics gave me a sedative. I don't remember crossing the Atlantic, or landing in Paris. Only vaguely do I remember speeding along in a French ambulance, the siren sounding different from ours, the conversation something you might be able to understand if the world would just slow down for a minute and let you think about it.

Another hospital, another room. Maggie there, faithful and tired, smelling like she needed a bath. Examinations, machine scans, patches. Then sleep.

But only briefly. I woke abruptly, and the room was dim. Apparently hospital half-light at night is universal. Or maybe it was just my half-blindness. . . . The shape of Maggie sprawled in a chair by my bedside, snoring softly.

I didn't wake her. Instead I fumbled for the call button and pressed it. Instead of a program, I got a live nurse as first response—something an American hospital could never have afforded. She was a soft white blur.

"*M'sieur?*"

"*Il me faut téléphoner.*"

"*Non, non. Pas de téléphone.*"

"*Oui! Un téléphone maintenant!*" I lowered my voice, not wanting to involve Maggie, who would have refused to let me become involved either.

"*Non.*" The tone was final. But also kind.

"*Alors, vous . . . téléphonez-vous à mon fils John. . . .*" I was losing strength. "*S'il vous plaît! Pour l'amour de Dieu!*"

I don't know why I added that. Some forgotten echo of melodramatic French literature . . . I was not thinking clearly. But the nurse moved closer and said softly, a whisper through the darkness, "*M'sieur? Vous etes christien? Je téléphonerai à votre fils.*"

She would do it. I got out, "*Téléphonez 301-555-7986 . . . Ditez-vous à John, 'Allez-vous à 593 Skinner Street . . . rue Skinner . . . Billy McCullough . . . pour l'enfant . . . pour l'enfant pour Laurie.' . . .*"

There was no way she could have absorbed all that, all those numbers. And I couldn't repeat it. The drugs were claiming me again, the drugs were the reason I wanted to call John in the first place. . . . Laurie couldn't go see Billy McCullough, it was too dangerous. It would have to be John. . . . No, John couldn't do it, my son was too ineffectual. . . . I couldn't think. The room was slipping away. "Mam'selle . . . s'il vous plait . . ."

"Restez tranquille, m'sieur. Dormez-vous."

John couldn't handle it . . . all those numbers . . . had I even said them in French, I wasn't sure I had. . . .

"Dormez-vous."

I slept.

16

SHANA WALDERS

The van speeds up, like we've turned onto an expressway. I pull frantically against my chain but it don't come loose from the side of the van. The tape across my mouth is so tight I can hardly make even a tiny noise. All I can do is sit there, like meat.

I'm so scared my back teeth rattle.

"Well?" Emily Jogerst says to the guy with the computer. He's studying the screen. "Is she in NCIS?"

"Duffy hasn't answered yet. . . . Wait, here it comes. Yup, she's there. Her name's Shana Walders. Sealed juvenile records, an arrest for petty larceny, let go with a warning . . . wait. Oh, boy."

"What?" Jogerst says.

"She was arraigned for criminal trespass with attempted assault. Her court date is next month."

"So?"

"The assault was at the International Center. On Cameron Atuli."

Jogerst lets out a long breath. "You're sure?"

"That's what Duffy's sending me."

"I see."

Jogerst looks at me hard. She's thinking. Finally she says, "Truth drugs don't work well with sedatives, Shana. So I'm not going to knock you out. You just sit there and

think about what you're going to tell us when we get where
we're going."

Eventually the van stops and I think I might get a chance
to run, or fight, or something when they take the manacles
off. But they're very professional. The van parks in a small
underground lot and I'm hustled through a heavy-security
door on the same level, and I don't get no chance to kick
nobody. They manacle me to a chair that's screwed to the
floor. The room is windowless and dusty, with stained
foamcast walls. There isn't nothing in it except more chairs
and a vidcam. Jogerst sits in another chair, legs crossed,
and waits. A man comes in with a patch. I try to squirm
away as he slaps it onto my neck, but it's hopeless. After he
leaves, Jogerst rips the tape off my mouth. It hurts like
hell.

"Now, tell me about every encounter you've ever had
with Cameron Atuli, Nicholas Clementi, Billy McCullough, and Laurie Clementi. Tell them in the order they
happened, and don't leave anything out."

"Fuck you!"

She sighs. "No. That patch was a truth drug, you know.
You don't have a choice, Shana."

And I don't. I feel something taking over my brain, and
from a long distance away I hear her repeat her orders.
Then I hear myself answering, and even while the real
Shana is screaming inside me, I can't stop myself. I tell her
everything.

Afterwards, I must of slept—the truth drugs do that to
you. Fitful sleep, because I'm still manacled in the chair. I
doze, wake, hear myself cry out. It could be the middle of

the night, or even the next morning. I doze again. And I dream.

It's one of them weird dreams with no people, but you know the people are there someplace, just out of sight. I'm standing in a big white room with hundreds of pedestals in it like the pedestal Maggie has between her French doors to hold a bowl of fresh flowers. Only Maggie's pedestal is made of greenish marble, and these are all white. On top of each pedestal is a cock fucking a cunt. No people—just a cut-off cock hanging in mid-air while it humps a cut-off pussy lying on the pedestal. Erect and hard and thrusting away, cocks and cunts row after row after row, jerking and pumping mindless and mutilated, coming again and again. . . .

I scream and the scream wakes me. After that, I can't sleep at all. I just sit and try to breathe.

A long time later, the lights flash on and fresher air streams into the room. Jogerst comes in with two big men, one of them the guy from the van. "Okay," she says, "take her to—"

"Emily," another voice says. "I just heard."

He's little and ugly, but everyone else turns instantly to where he stands in the doorway. "How bad is it?"

"Not as bad as I feared, Doctor," Jogerst says. "The tape is ready for you to review. But she's nobody, just a kid with a private grudge. She saw the product after the lab detonation in Lanham. But nobody believed her then, and nobody knows she contacted me except Cameron Atuli, and he doesn't have any means to follow her. He'll go to Clementi, of course, and then maybe to the police."

"No problem. I doubt they'd even believe him. She's got priors and he's induced retrograde amnesia, right?"

"Yes," Jogerst says. "Do you think we should call Leonard?"

"No. The fewer details we force on him, the less uneasy he is."

"What about calling—"

"I already took care of that. I don't see a real problem, here, Emily. Certainly nothing locale-shifting. But you're right, I'll want to review the tape before I make a final decision."

Jogerst nods, and they go out, leaving me manacled there.

Leonard. I know that name from someplace. But is it Leonard Somebody or Somebody Leonard?

It's maybe another hour before anyone comes back, and this time it's the guy from the van. He's got hot eyes and hotter hands. He grins as he unlocks me.

"Where are you taking me?"

"You don't want to know," he says, but he's one of the kind that wants me to know. Everything. He gets off on it.

Real casual, he gets me in a lock with my arm up behind my back. A little more pressure and the arm will break. He takes me out of the dusty, stuffy room, which now I'd give anything to stay in, and down a hallway. At another door he stops.

"You want to see something hot, pretty bitch? Of *course* you do."

I want to spit in his face, but I'm afraid he'll break my arm. I don't say nothing. He keys in a door code, drags me through, and releases my arm.

I stagger and almost faint.

I'm facing a wall of glass or plastic so transparent that I'm only sure it's there because my hands hit it when I lurch forward. Behind the glass is a lab, with three medical types in white coats and masks. On the lab benches, wired to computers, are pieces of people.

Kids' heads, some almost whole and some just patches of skin stretched over a mesh frame. A patch of baby skull, part of a nose, the left half of a mouth.

Tiny little kids' hands, looking like they've had fingers cut off.

Pieces of underskin, bloody and raw.

"Appetizing, huh?" the computer guy says. He jerks my head down to make sure I see the half-a-baby skull with one eye, close to the glass wall. But it isn't no kids' heads that make me almost faint.

On the side wall, behind another glass, is a second lab. I can see it clearly. Inside is my dream.

Not exactly. No humping cocks. But on rows of white counters, floating in some kind of liquid inside clear boxes, are cunts. More than cunts—whole female pelvises, from the waist to the tops of the thighs. The places where the legs and upper bodies got cut off are covered with some kind of stretchy white material. The pussies are all shaved clean. And the bellies bulge—some a little, some a lot. The floating pelvises are all pregnant.

The blond guy sees where I'm looking. He whispers hot in my ear. "You fertile, pretty bitch? Because the doc don't know how to make artificial wombs. Or maybe he does, and this is just cheaper. Take the ovaries, the tubes, the uterus, the birth canal. Fuck it with an artificial insemination tube. Let the embryo grow right where it was meant to. . . . After that there's plenty of customers, of course.

All those women who can't have kids. Suddenly—a mira-cle! She's carrying a fetus! And nobody knows where she got it, sometimes not even the husband. . . . Of course, they want pretty babies, and that means starting with pretty cunts full of pretty eggs. . . ."

I start to scream. Instantly Emily Jogerst is beside me. "Ben, you stupid brute . . . get her into the other lab! We don't have time for your perverse jollies!"

"Sorry, Em." He puts the arm lock on me again and drags me away. I can't stop screaming.

It doesn't matter. They strap me, wrists and ankles, on-to a bed. I can't even move my head. Oh Jesus God no don't . . . don't cut . . .

But they only slide the bed inside a big tank. Total dark-ness. Machinery reaches out and gently grips my head. I can't move it even a tiny bit. Even my lips are held firmly in one position by something that faintly tingles. But noth-ing hurts me.

I'm not claustrophobic.

Was Atuli? This is a MOSS tank. They're taking scans of the cells in my skin, layer by layer. I remember what Nick told me. The scans take hours.

And then?

Next comes tissue samples. Tissue samples of blood, skin, hair, lips . . . will that hurt?

And then? *Of course, they want pretty babies, and that means starting with* . . .

I can't help it. Inside the tank, even though I can't move my mouth, I start screaming again, and it comes out a strangled gurgle like I'm already in the middle of dying.

17

CAMERON ATULI

A matinee performance, and Shana still has not called.

We're dancing in our own small theater at Aldani House, a benefit performance for some elderly-charity. It's a matinee because the rich patrons, all of them ancient themselves, probably have to be in bed by 8:00 P.M. I stand in the wings as they totter in and fill the seats with antique lace, with black tie at two in the afternoon, with silk cleverly cut to cover a dowager hump. People like that want a flashy program, full of spectacle: we're dancing sections from *Western Symphony*, *Firebird*, and *Salvadore*. Sarah passes me, dressed in a fantastic holo of red and orange feathers; Tasha in a saloon-girl tutu and black lace mitts; Alonso in a blood-soaked tights of brown-green camouflage. The small orchestra tunes up with the usual discordant yawling. On stage, behind the opaqued curtain, the resin rises in illuminated clouds as dancers warm up. I should be out there, but my concentration is gone. All I can think of is that Shana Walders has not called.

After twenty-four hours go to Nick Clementi, she said. It's been nineteen hours. And a half. But Shana wouldn't need all twenty-four to talk to Emily Jogerst, would she? And as soon as they'd talked, Shana would call to let me know she's safe, wouldn't she?

Maybe not. Maybe the stupid girl forgot that I'm here worrying that she's . . . I can't think about it.

"Cam?" Rob, in jeans and cowboy hat for *Western Symphony.* "Are you warmed up?"

"Yes. No. Rob—" I haven't told him about Shana's trip to Philadelphia. Protecting him, I guess. From what? Neither of us has to risk the trip to Philadelphia. Or would. I didn't like the idea in the first place, but there was no stopping Shana Walders.

"What is it, Cam?"

"Nothing. Go on; there's your call."

The dancers for *Western Symphony* take their places, and the curtain goes up.

By the second selection, when I must remove my wrister to dance Prince Ivan in *Firebird,* Shana still hasn't called. Nor is there any message when I rush offstage, sweating and panting, after my *pas de deux* is finished. Sarah follows me. "What's wrong, Cam? You were way off tonight. I thought you were going to drop me on that last lift!"

"I'm sorry. I . . . I don't feel well. Listen, could you explain to Mr. C. that I couldn't make curtain call? That I had to go lie down?"

She stares at me. I know I don't look ill. And curtain call is important at a benefit like this . . . the patrons want their considerable money's worth. They want to stand and shout *Bravo!* and see roses delivered to Sarah and Caroline: the entire show. I don't dare skip curtain call, in costume and full makeup. I just don't dare.

So it's nearly six in the evening when I reach Dr. Clementi's in Bethesda. I ring the bell over and over, but no one answers, not even a house system. Finally I use the duplicate key Shana gave me to let myself in. I search the library, the living room, the master bedroom, Shana's room. But there's no note, no recorded message, nothing left by the family to tell Shana where Dr. and Mrs. Clementi went or when they'd be back.

I can't think what to do next, so I do nothing. I sit in the library and wait. Someone has to come home, sometime.

And what's happening to Shana in the meantime?

Finally, desperate, I press the vid button beside "Laurie Clementi." That's who Shana is supposed to be. Although I can't think how I'm going to explain to Laurie who *I* am, or why I'm in her father-in-law's house. . . .

"Please leave a message for this number," a system voice says. "Thank you." I cut off.

I don't know who else to call. Except for the people at Aldani House, and Dr. Newell, I remember no one else in the world.

The phone rings. The house system answers, and then Dr. Clementi's voice, thank heavens. *"Téléphonez 301-555-7986 . . . Ditez-vous à John, 'Allez-vous à 593 Skinner Street . . . rue Skinner . . . Billy McCullough . . . pour l'enfant . . . pour l'enfant pour Laurie.' . . ."*

Why is Dr. Clementi speaking French? And to whom? Not to John—he's telling someone else to call John. "Repeat," I say, although I understood the words the first time. French is one of the languages I don't know how I know. The system repeats the message, which makes no more sense this time.

Who is Billy McCullough? Does he know where Shana is now? There's no one home at John Clementi's, I just called. I glance at the time: 7:02.

What I need to do is send police to this Skinner Street address, because if "Billy McCullough" is connected with a baby for Laurie Clementi, then he might also be connected to Emily Jogerst. But I don't know any police; I don't know anyone. And Shana told me that the woman who talked to me at the New York gala, the old-lady patron, was really an FBI agent—also that the police had rescued me from the people who abducted me but then kept the whole thing quiet, with no prosecution. Protecting the criminals. Which police can I trust? Any of them?

I know nothing, nothing. It's all been deleted. And I chose this ignorance for myself, rather than live with what was done to me. But I haven't escaped that unknown past after all. Here it is, pressing in all around me.

All that my operation did was wipe away the knowledge that might have helped me now. I crippled myself. I, myself. Or was I really the one who even chose the operation? I don't know. I can't remember.

In sudden fury, I activate the vid system and leave a message at Laurie Clementi's house, right after her father's: "Dr. Clementi, this is Cameron Atuli. I just got your message, the French one, to John. He's not there and he's not at your house either, where I am now. Shana is missing. So I'm going to go myself to meet Billy McCullough and tell him you said . . ." What? I didn't know what sort of baby deal was being arranged for Laurie Clementi—although surely it had to be secret. But this is all I have to keep these people from hurting Shana. ". . . going to tell Billy McCullough that you said that Shana Walders is being followed by the authorities, and they should be careful to have nothing to do with her. Or the whole structure could fall through." Whatever it was.

Then I stand in the middle of the Clementi library and fight the rising panic. I have to do this. I have to go to Skinner Street and talk to someone who might have been involved in my own kidnapping and in my. . . . But I *have* to do this. If I don't, Shana may die. I can't just wipe the situation out of mind.

I try to think ahead, to plan: money from an ATM, call a cab at the crossing two blocks down, convincing lies to tell Billy McCullough. A weapon? I search the house, watching the time. In Shana's room I find a military stun gun that she probably isn't supposed to have. I don't know how it works, but I experiment for a few minutes until I think I've got it.

Then I leave the house quietly, closing the front door as if it might break, locking it gently because my hands are trembling and I think that otherwise I might drop and lose my fragile hold on the stolen key.

Skinner Street is just an alley running between the numbered streets a dozen blocks off the Mall in D.C. This is a different world from Bethesda. Garbage blows across the narrow street, lined on both sides with crumbling walls of brick and rotted wood. Boards cover about a third of the storefronts and narrow doors; the rest are barred. In the summer twilight people loiter outside, glaring at each other: a dangerous-looking black man rooting in a garbage can, a prostitute in a red skirt and gold holo wig, three old people in bent metal lawn chairs in the middle of the sidewalk. No kids. The air smells of cooking and broken toilets.

A rat walks across the concrete stoop of 346. I jump back. It stops and stares at me insolently, completely unafraid, before finishing its walk and disappearing into a crack in the building foundation. I wait for a minute before taking its place on the stoop and knocking on the door. It rings faintly, solid metal.

"I'm here to see Billy McCullough," I say to the woman who opens the door a crack, chain fastened. She's old, with thin gray hair and skin the color of mine, but seamed in hundreds of crisscrossing lines. Behind her is a tiny living room with sagging sofa, new bright green rug, heavy green curtains tightly drawn. "Dr. Nicholas Clementi sent me."

She removes the chain, unsmiling. "Come in."

"I'll wait here," I say, half inside and half on the concrete stoop. "Ask him to come here, please."

She shrugs and shuffles off, into another room or maybe a hallway. Voices rise and fall, but I can't distinguish any words. Then an old white man in an expensive suit comes into the room, sees me, and stops dead.

"Holy God." He stares as if I'm a ghost. "Who the fuck are you?"

"Dr. Clementi sent me," I say, and manage to keep my voice level. "About the baby for his daughter-in-law Laurie. He couldn't come himself, he's too sick, but he said I should give you an extremely important message. He said —"

"Halleck!" McCullough calls, and instantly another man appears beside McCullough. This one takes one look at me and says, "The face on the monkeys!" and draws a gun.

I fumble in my vest for Shana's gun but I'm nowhere near fast enough. The other man's stunner hits me in the legs and instantly they're gone, vanished, I can't feel them at all and I'm flat on the concrete stoop outside. My legs, I have to have my legs I can't dance without legs. . . .

"That's enough, Halleck! I have to be able to fucking question him! Get him inside!"

My legs are still there, I can see them. I just can't move them at all. Shana's gun is wrenched from my hand and someone grabs me under the armpits and drags me inside the house. I twist the top half of my body to fight, but without the bottom half I can't get any leverage. So I grab both sides of the doorway and brace myself hard.

"Get him loose! Get him *in* here!"

He can't get me loose; I'm hanging onto the door jamb with all the strength I developed for lifting ballerinas.

Halleck curses, lets go of my armpits, and brings both his hands locked together onto my belly.

The pain is astonishing. And I can't breathe, I can't get any *air*. . . . He's dragging me inside and I'm going to suffocate because I can't get any air. . . . I can't even scream, I can't do anything—something heavy falls on top of me, and I'm struggling so hard to simply breathe that it's long agonizing moments before I realize it's Halleck.

The concrete stoop is boiling with people, dragging Halleck's body off me and leaping over me into the room and shouting. It's moments more before enough painful air fills my lungs so that I can sort out the sounds. The old gray-haired woman cawing obscenities; people shouting on the street behind me; the dangerous-looking black bum from beside the garbage can bending over me.

"Police, Atuli. You all right?"

"P . . . p . . . p . . ." I still don't have enough air in my lungs to talk.

"Yeah, police. We followed you."

I must look baffled because he smiles reluctantly and says, "You never guessed that Dr. Clementi's phone's monitored? Kind of naive to be doing this, ain't you?"

Shana would have guessed. Shana would have used a public phone to call John. Shana . . .

"Shana . . . Walders!" I gasp. My lungs feel shredded; every word hurts. "They've . . . got her! They'll—"

"No, they won't," the cop says grimly. "Not if McCullough talks quick enough."

McCullough—they must have taken him somewhere. Outside, or to the back of the house. I can't ask; I can't talk any more. The cop tries to help me to my feet, but I still have no legs. The stunner. Finally he lifts me in his huge arms and dumps me on the sagging sofa.

"It'll wear off in fifteen minutes. Meanwhile, just stay there." He vanishes into the back of the house. The prostitute in the short red skirt—another cop?—follows him, and a third person goes out the front door and closes it behind him.

All of a sudden I'm alone.

Not if McCullough talks quick enough. I lie back and close my eyes, trying not to think, not to picture what could happen if McCullough doesn't give them the address of Emily Jogerst's operation in Philadelphia, or doesn't know it. . . . Oh dear God won't it ever end . . . ?

A noise in the room, followed by a gasp and running feet. I open my eyes. Standing by my sofa, looking at me from dark steady eyes, is a small child that is me.

My face, my eyes, my skin. But the little boy's thick hair is black and straight, cut in long bangs, which makes him look faintly Asian. He wears red overalls and a T-shirt with blue rabbits. We stare at each other, and my heart stops. Then the child pulls back his lips to show solid square monkey teeth, chitters loudly, and scampers across the room to climb the green curtains with his human hands and hairy, curving, prehensile feet.

"Come back, dammit!" says the red-skirted prosti-
tute/cop. She reaches up toward the chimp, who chitters at
her from my face and then suddenly leaps at her. It wraps
its arms around her neck and cuddles its head into her
breast. She holds it fast and hurries from the room.

I can't go after them. I can't move. All I can do is what I
am doing: look down the hall where the chimp-me disappeared into some other place, far out of my reach.

18

SHANA WALDERS

By the time they take me out of the MOSS tank, I've got a plan. I've had hours in there to think, hours strapped down in the total dark.

What I think is that I don't want to be cut up and turned into a cunt-and-womb baby-maker.

And I don't want a Shana face on bunches of chimps, neither. I'm me, the only me, and I'm a human being, even if I've been a stupid arrogant bitch to get myself into this position. But there's no use crying about the past; what counts is what I do when they take me out of the tank. So I think up a plan. My head is completely immobile, and my wrists and ankles are tightly strapped down and won't budge. I have to use the only thing I can still control.

"All right, Shana. Stage two." Emily Jogerst is right there when my bed is rolled out from inside the tank. She's standing close, next to the short ugly doctor in a white coat, plus a black man and a young girl. Those two pull out my stretcher. They're in jeans. I see everyone clearly but they don't know that because my eyes are wide and fixed in my rigid face. Then the smell hits them.

"Oh, God, she's shit herself," the girl says. "Catatonic shock."

"So clean her up," Jogerst says. "And drug her for the tissue samples. Call me when you're done." She leaves the room. After a minute, the short ugly doctor follows her, wrinkling his nose.

"Lucky us," the girl mutters. "God, she stinks. Unstrap her, Larry."

Larry unstraps my wrists. The girl goes over to a sink and I hear water running. Larry moves to the foot of my stretcher and unstraps my ankles.

I jerk to a sit and thrust both hands under Maggie's blue dress. Hours of wriggling against the stretcher mattress rubbed my bikini panties down to my knees; there's nothing in my way. I grab a handful of my shit and throw it right in Larry's face.

He jumps backward and cries out, which is not the right thing to do. Shit gets into his mouth and the next minute he's retching. I'm gagging myself but I still leap off the bed and rush to the girl, who's holding a water basin, eyes wide. I grab the basin and smack her over the head with it. That holds her while I reach for something better, which turns out to be a heavy metal piece of equipment, God knows what it's really for. I bash her with a sharp metal corner and she goes down. I turn to Larry.

He roars like a charging rhino and comes at me. I drop the metal thing and meet him with both hands thrust out front, and I've slimed them good. He can't help it. With the taste of shit filling his mouth and smeared across his face, he can't help himself—he hesitates a second. It's enough. His charge is broken, and I duck under and tackle him, bringing him down with me on top. I shove one hand toward his eyes, and while he closes them and jerks his head to the side to avoid me, I've got time to grab with the other hand for the sharp metal where I dropped it on the floor. I hit him in the neck, and then on the head, and I keep hitting him until he doesn't move.

Then I'm up, panting, reeking like a sewer. There's a knife on the counter. It's wicked sharp. I try not to think what it was for, and I move with it toward the door.

The door isn't locked. On the other side is the hallway Jogerst brought me down hours ago, the hallway that leads past the lab with—

I move down the hallway with my back to the wall, toward the dusty windowless room where the entrance is.

I never reach it. Suddenly there's an explosion. I hit the ground. People shout. And the hallway is filled with cops in full body armor and computerized weapons.

Atuli. Went to Nick, who went for the cops. Atuli actually came through.

"Freeze!" a cop yells at me, and I lie my cheek against the hard floor and thank my Irish luck that that rucky-fucky dancer had some balls after all.

19

NICK CLEMENTI

It's like a lion at the door;
And when the door begins to crack,
It's like a stick across your back;
And when your back begins to smart,
It's like a penknife in your heart;
And when your heart begins to bleed,
You're dead, and dead, and dead, indeed.

Only I wasn't.

"It's so wonderful," Maggie said, the nurses said, the French doctors leading the clinical trial said, proudly. "So wonderful." And it was. I'd responded well to the French experimental drug. The mucormycosis organisms in my sinuses died obediently. The fibers grown into my brain and optic nerves ceased reproducing and became necrotic tissue, to be removed by phagocytes. The damage already done to my nerve tissue could not, of course, be repaired. My balance was slightly impaired; I would walk for the rest of my life with a cane. Vision was dimmed in both eyes. There had been some damage to my olfactory nerves, and smells had to be quite strong for me to detect them. But I was not going to die.

It was wonderful. Everybody said so.

Then why did I feel this pervasive sense of sadness, of futility? Day after day I sat in my cheery French hospital room, talked with Maggie, worked with the physical therapy computers, grew stronger and healthier. And all the while, the sadness and futility grew in my mind, as once the mucormycosis fibers had grown so relentlessly in my brain.

Stress, the doctors said, with our century's relentless eagerness to assign all things to neurotransmitters. *Depression*. In other words, I was depressed because I felt depression, stressed because I was under stress. No one seemed to consider this tautological.

I wanted more.

What more, for sweet pity's sake? What more could a man ask than that he be handed back his life? There was no greater gift than that.

Sallie called every day from Atlanta, and Laurie from Washington, and even, once, Alana from Mars. Old friends sent good wishes. And John called, his aggrieved sulkiness hidden under concern for me, but not hidden very well. "I got your message about the meeting with 'Billy McCullough,' about a—"

"About something confidential," I said quickly.

"Yeah. Why didn't you tell me you were doing . . . that?"

"I was doing it for Laurie," I said. I laid my head back on my pillows and closed my eyes, but John's image on the vidscreen went on talking anyway.

"You might have told *me*."

"Sorry. Did you go to the meeting with McCullough?"

"No. I didn't get the message in time. Why did you call your house instead of mine? That would have been the sensible thing to do."

"Because I was drugged."

"Oh. Is that why you spoke in French?"

"I spoke to the nurse in French. . . ." But it was too much effort to explain. If John heard my own voice on the answering system, speaking in French, then it could only be because the nurse wore a recording device and had replayed it verbatim. That was common in terminal cases, to analyze speech patterns later and so deduce brain activity. It must have been how she got the phone number and house number accurately.

"So what do I do now about this McCullough?" John said. "Dad, are you even listening to me?"

"No," I said. "I'm tired. Goodbye, son." McCullough must have waited for me a while at the restaurant and then left. I would have to contact him again and start the process over when I got home, if I wanted to. I should, of course; every time Laurie called on vid I could see the white strain on her face, the unhappiness, the maternal longing she tried to hide. She'd lost even more weight; her cheek and collar bones protruded like chisels. I should send a message to Billy McCullough that I was still interested. But somehow, I couldn't find the emotional energy.

"Let's go sit on the bench outside," Maggie said, her sharp worried eyes on me. "There are some wonderful red flower-things in bloom." Maggie was a gardener, but not a genetic botanist.

"You go, sweetheart," I said. "I think I need a nap." And I would lie in bed, feigning sleep to avoid talk, despising myself for not appreciating what had been given back to me.

What *had* been given back to me?

I was old. That had not changed. The old must be prepared to die, and I had made my peace with death. And now there was no death, at least not yet. I had fought a battle within myself, and won peace, and now it turned out that my victory was only over an enemy who hadn't been present on the battlefield in the first place.

And eventually I would have to do it all over again.

I wasn't depressed. I was *angry*. I had accepted death, and death had not accepted me, and I didn't know if I had the courage to again meet the enemy with dignity and grace. To do it all over again . . .

And everyone went around saying, "Isn't it wonderful!" and any rational mind had to agree that it was. Reprieved from a fatal disease. Snatched from the jaws of death.

Only to have them snap down on me again, probably soon, because I was still old and I was still running out of time. But I couldn't say that to anyone, not even Maggie. It was too ungrateful, too obvious, too whining. All I could do was lie with my eyes closed, or stare out the hospital window, and know that, with the perversity of human beings, I was now more afraid of dying than I had been when I thought I was actually doing it.

"Dr. Bourdeloue, je voudrais aller chez moi."

The doctor smiled, probably more at my accent than at my desire to return home. *"Pourquoi?"*

"Parce que . . . seulement parce que." Because.

In his silence I heard disappointment. I was not properly uplifted by his miracle. But finally he said philosophically, *"Oui. Ce n'est pas defendu. Allez-vous chez vous."*

"I can leave," I said to Maggie.

"Do you want to leave?"

"Why not?" Now that the doctor had agreed, I found it didn't really matter to me. Like everything else.

"Do you want to *not* leave?"

"Why not?" I said, and tried to smile. She sat close enough to my bedside to see her expression; she didn't smile back. Her dress was bright, screaming green, a color

Maggie never wore. She must have bought new clothes in Paris, brighter clothes, so that I could more easily follow her movements. Her voice was steel.

"Okay, Nick, let's have this out."

"Maggie . . . don't push."

"I haven't been," she said. "But I am now. What is wrong? There's something you're not telling me!"

"No, I . . . no."

"Don't lie to me, Nick! God, I almost lost you, and now I've got you back again, and don't you dare push me away by lying to me! What aren't you telling me?"

"Sounds like there's a lot he hasn't told you yet," a deep, rich voice said from the doorway.

Vanderbilt Grant.

Maggie blinked, but I found I wasn't all that surprised. Maybe at some level I'd been expecting him. Or maybe surprise, like everything else, seemed pointless.

"Hello, Maggie. Nick, I flew over especially to talk to you. Maggie, you may as well stay. I know Nick will end up telling you everything anyway, sooner or later."

After that statement, dislodging Maggie would have been like moving Gibraltar. Her green dress jerked, then settled more firmly back into her chair, removing her expression beyond my vision. Nor could I see Van's expression, but the outline of his big body seemed to have changed. He stooped, and his shoulders sagged. I wasn't sure, but I thought his right hand trembled, a twitching blur. Stress? Disease? Or just old age?

All I could think about was old age.

Maggie said, "*What* hasn't Nick told me so far, Van? And why not?"

I said wearily, "He hasn't told you that this clinical trial didn't just happen to turn up when I just happened to be *in extremis.* Did it, Van? The timing was too coincidental."

Van said nothing. He moved closer to my bed.

"As Commissioner of the FDA," I said, "you knew perfectly well that this experimental drug was being tested in Paris. And you knew, because you made it your business to find out, that I was being treated for mucormycosis. But you didn't arrange for me to come here until you wanted me out of the country."

Maggie paled, half rose from her chair, sat down again. Van's stooped form dropped heavily into a chair at the foot of my bed. I still couldn't see his expression.

"Try to understand, Nick," his deep musical voice said. "The unusually high success rate of the mucormycosis drug wasn't validated until just a few weeks ago. That part *was* a coincidence. You know what most clinical trials are. The new drugs are usually only marginally more effective than whatever was being used before. Until those results came in to my office, chances are you would have traveled a far distance, had a lot of extra pain, and probably died anyway. It wasn't a choice between saving your life or letting you die. It was a choice between prolonging your dying or letting you slip away more quickly. Or so I thought."

"And you wanted me to 'slip away' more quickly. You wanted me in a coma as soon as possible. Why, Van?"

I hadn't expected him to answer. But he did, and I glimpsed again the huge contradictions in the man, the inner wars he must have fought all his complicated life.

"I wanted you to go quickly because I didn't want you investigating Shana Walders, or Cameron Atuli, or Billy McCullough."

For the first time, I realized that my hospital room door

was closed. No nurses passed in and out. I was late for physical therapy, but no French orderly in cheerful red-and-blue had come to wheel me to the machines. Van had arranged for durable privacy. He must have considerable pull behind him to do that. And considerable motivation, to cross the ocean in his condition, whatever it was.

I said slowly, "You know why I was going to Billy Mc-Cullough. You know because the FDA knows what the vivifacturers are doing. The chimps, the kidnappings . . . all of it. You know. You permit it."

"Not the kidnapping. Of course not that. And you have to understand, we don't know about *any* of it, not officially. We never deal directly with those people. We sub-contract with independent testing labs and—"

"And *they* contract with the illegal vivifacturers. And when you discover it, you work hard at looking the other way. The government as a whole works hard at looking the other way. That's why Shana Walders's testimony about the chimps with Atuli's face was buried in Committee in the first place . . . *that's* why the FBI was so eager to let Atuli have the retrograde-induced amnesia. . . . My God."

"Nick—" Van's voice said, and it was a plea.

"But why? Why, Van? It can't be that President Combes is tolerating all this just to—*does* Combes know? Does the Surgeon General? The CDC?"

"I can't answer any of those questions," Van said. Maggie sat like stone, a motionless green blur.

I said, "Of course they know. Unofficially. That's why they were onto Sallie so fast and hard when she accessed Atuli's name—"

"We'll fix that," Van said. "Sallie can be reinstated. Somebody acted too precipitously."

Maggie choked out, "Do you know what you're admitting to, Van?" and Van suddenly came to life, his old self. No—his young self. He raised his right hand, and its tremor had disappeared. His voice swelled with the oratory that had won him embattled streets, Harvard debates, courtroom victories, governmer . deadlocks. He couldn't help the oratory. Words were both his natural weapons and his natural shield.

"Yes, Maggie—I know what I'm admitting to. The toleration of law-breaking. More—the toleration of evil. Nothing less than that. You see, I believe in evil. I've seen enough it in a life I sometimes think has seen too much, gone on too long. I admit to tolerating the illegal vivifacturers. I admit to looking the other way when they do evil. I admit to protecting them. I admit to doing everything in my not inconsiderable power to get my government to tolerate them, to look the other way when they do evil, and to even protect them. Yes—*protect* brutal criminals. And do you know why? Do you, Maggie?"

Did he even know he was playing to her, not me? Wooing her, as if she were a TV camera, or a voting bloc? I didn't think he knew. Impassioned, convoluted, manipulative, and utterly sincere—he just barreled ahead.

"You're asking yourself, Maggie, why would any head of the FDA let vivifacture violations go on and on? Why would Vanderbilt Grant? Why would all the people he's persuaded? Not in order to give a few hundred childless couples chimpanzee or puppy babies with a ballet dancer's face. Not to keep the press spotlight off aging society matrons who grow themselves fresh new facial skin from their relatively unwithered belly cells. Not to allow the black market in infants to operate unchecked, to get around the gene-pool regulations. Not for any of those reasons."

Lying in my bed, I watched him, fascinated even though I couldn't see him clearly. Van was up and pacing now, but "pacing" didn't describe it. He was a geyser, barely contained in the little room.

"Maggie, the FDA tolerates and protects those vivifacturers—*Vanderbilt Grant* tolerates and protects them—because they're the only ones doing basic genetic research that might solve the sperm-count crisis at its root. They're the only ones who *can* do that research. In our zeal to protect the American people, we've strangled all other DNA-level research with regulations, constraints, prohibitions—and then on top of that, we cut off the funding. We *had* to. There's no money. There's a spirit of caution in the citizens. 'Don't risk anything! We've lost too much already! Conserve and preserve! Don't take chances!' And all the while . . . all the while . . ."

His words caught, broke off. Deliberately? He stopped pacing and stood still in front of Maggie's chair, and in the treacherously beautiful voice I thought I heard genuine sadness.

"All the while, Maggie, only the criminals have been engaged in the basic research that might yet save us. Into DNA-level cures for sperm count. Into counteragents for what the synthetic chemicals have done to our endocrine systems—you didn't know that, did you, Nick? You thought you were the only one looking seriously at that data. But the illegal labs are. Out of greed, of course, in hopes of making a fortune . . . but they're doing it. The criminals are the ones conducting the financially risky investigations. The ones committing the resources. The ones making the dangerous experiments biology needs to yield up answers. Only the criminals have dared.

"The rest of us . . . the rest of us just want to play it safe. The rest of us are just too old."

Van finished. Maggie—not usually a pushover audience—leaned forward until her face again swam into my view. She gazed at Van in awe, in fury, in compassion. No one spoke.

Then, finally, Van turned toward me. "Nick . . . I know what I did to you. To that National Service girl, Shana Walders. I know what was done to Cameron Atuli, that the government could have prosecuted for and instead covered up. But now you know why I did it, and now I have to ask your help."

He paused—for effect? But his right hand trembled again, and when I caught a spasm in his arm as well, I was sure. Savoye's Disease, in its first stages. The myelin sheaths around Vanderbilt Grant's nerve cells were rapidly degenerating. There was no cure. Nothing we've researched can regenerate nerve cells—at least, nothing we've researched legally.

Savoye's Disease is one of the neurological disorders triggered by synthetic endocrine disrupters.

"It's not easy keeping security on something like this," Van said. "Not easy keeping the press away, not easy keeping smart scientists and politicians from asking questions—like you did, Nick. We've succeeded so far only because whenever anyone had evidence that the illegal labs were being protected, we've been able to bring them in with us. Scientists, independent testing labs, drug companies—it's to their advantage to work with us. Nobody who could harm us couldn't be persuaded."

"You mean 'bought,' " I said, and he had the honesty to not deny it.

"Possibly. If what one is buying is hope for the human race, perhaps salvation from our own folly that—"

"No more rhetoric, please, Van," Maggie said tartly, and I saw that she had recovered from his oratorical onslaught. "Now you think evidence has been uncovered by some people who can't be bought. Or, if they are bought, couldn't be trusted about the quality of their silence."

He said simply, "Yes."

She said, "Then why not just kill them?"

"Maggie!" I gasped.

"I'm making a point, Nick. Van says the government is screwing around with illegal vivifacture labs because it's our only practical hope for a way to evade results of our endocrine disrupter carelessness. He says the government knows the illegal vivifacturers are criminal, even evil in some of what they do, and he's willing to tolerate that for the rest of what they do. Then why not tolerate murder of witnesses as well? What's the difference? You're already allowing the illegal labs to murder. That's what they'd have done to Cameron Atuli if the FBI hadn't stepped in just in time, isn't it?"

"But the FBI did step in," Van said. "Because we're *not* willing to tolerate murder."

"You think you can draw a line," Maggie said icily. "This much evil is okay, but no more. And you think you can force everyone else toe your line, right?"

"Yes!" Van suddenly roared. "Because we have to! Damn it, Maggie, my job is to get things done! And if the government combined with public opinion make it so this is the only way I *can* get them done, then I'll do and tolerate and enforce whatever the fuck I have to!"

"And you want Nick to tolerate it, too. That's why you're here, isn't it?" Maggie stood and faced Van, five-three to his six-four. "You're buying his silence. By saving his life. So that he'll control Shana Walders and Cameron Atuli and keep them quiet in ways you can't." A new thought occurred to her; she suddenly whirled on *me*, and so help me God I could feel the brief masculine twinge of relief in Van Grant's body.

"And what have *you* learned, Nick?" Maggie cried. "That you haven't told me, and apparently weren't going to?"

I looked at Vanderbilt Grant. It was hard to get the words out. I said, "That they're dead, aren't they? Maggie is wrong. Shana or Cameron, or both—they're already dead. They mucked around with your protected illegal vivifacturers, and got too close, and you—"

"No. They're not dead," Van said forcefully. "Maggie is right. Walders and Atuli are in protective custody. In isolation in a federal prison, but we can't keep them there too much longer. Your stupid kids got in too deep, and we had to go in after them or . . . we had to go in after them. *And we did.* We're not murderers, Nick, and it's a damn good thing we had your vidphone tapped. Atuli got your message about McCullough and tried to keep your appointment himself. . . . He's a brave kid. He—God, the stupid risks the young take!"

After a moment, he heard what he'd just said. *The stupid risks the young take*—the same stupid, life-threatening risks that the illegal labs were taking. Except that Shana and Cameron had apparently risked themselves, and the criminal labs only risked the lives of others.

But it was the lives of others—a whole country of others—that Van was fighting to give a chance at a reproductive future.

"Nick?" Van said. He was watching me closely.

"I'll think about it," I said. "About talking to Shana and Cameron. About securing their . . . silence. No promises, Van. But I'll think about it."

"How will I know your decision?" he said, suddenly humble. "And when? I can't hold them in prison much longer. There'll be civil-liberties lawyers all over me like maggots on carrion."

I thought about it. "Three days. Thursday. I want to talk to Shana and Atuli first. The doctors say I can go home; can you arrange for us to have immediate transport, and to visit the two kids wherever you've stashed them?"

Van nodded wordlessly and stood. He was still the master showman/politician—he knew the right moment to leave the stage. His footsteps echoed down the hospital corridor, and neither Maggie nor I spoke until the sound ended. Then she rose, walked to the window, and stared out. Even at that distance her green dress was bright to me, but her head and hands disappeared, ghost-like.

Into the strained silence she said suddenly, "Van's got some disease. His color is terrible. He's going to die."

"We're all going to die," I said, and even as I said the mock-cynical words, their truth smacked into me all over again. I could make peace with death all I wanted, or I could rage against it all I wanted, and neither would change anything. I was going to die, anyway, sooner or later, with or without dignity, with or without battlefield truces, with or without having arranged everything exactly as I wanted it. Life was too big for that sort of stage management. It was, in fact, an unfathomable series of messy risks, even for the old.

Especially for the old.

"Let's go home, Maggie. I've got some serious choices to make, and I'd rather make them at home."

She turned from the window and walked toward me. As her face rematerialized above the green dress, I saw that she was smiling. It wasn't until then, until Maggie smiled at me in that particular way, that I realized that, even though I hadn't chose to do so, I had fully rejoined the living for as long as I possibly could.

20

CAMERON ATULI

The prison cell has a concrete floor. It's actually a comfortable room, not at all what I thought a prison was like. Except for the locked metal door and lack of windows, it looks like a small hotel suite furnished without taste or imagination: beige rug and sofa, maple table and chairs with machine-lathe turnings, television, two beds in discreetly separate alcoves for Shana and me. The bathroom has a door. The silverware that comes with our meals includes bread knives.

"I could make a weapon out of any of a dozen things in here," Shana says with disgust. "There are coiled metal springs in that sofa, for God's sake!"

"And who would you use it on if you did?" I say acidly. She's really getting on my nerves. "In eight days, we haven't seen a single person." Our food trays arrive three times a day through a narrow slot. Nothing Shana has done—keeping the trays, not keeping the trays, wrecking one of the chairs, locking herself in the bathroom, pretending illness—has produced signs of any human being.

"God, Atuli, you're such a wimp. No one has shown up *yet*. That doesn't mean they won't. And I'm going to be ready for them, even if you'd rather just whine about what's under the rug."

"It's *concrete*," I say, but she only rolls her eyes. She's not stupid, but she acts it. The floor is concrete. It has no give at all. I can't dance on it without risking injury, and every day that goes by without dancing is a day for my muscles to stiffen and shorten.

I do what I can. I turn the sofa around, so the back faces the room, and I hold onto it to do two barres each day. *Pliés, battements, ronds de jambe, développés.* But I can't do any center work on this floor.

"And what if I want to actually sit on the sofa?" Shana asks, watching me scornfully.

"You can turn it back round when I'm done," I say. *Pliés, battements, ronds de jambe, développés.*

"I'm not a fucking furniture mover."

"Look, Shana," I say, "I know you hate being 'cooped up,' as you call it. But don't take it out on me. I'm busy."

"Yeah, right. Busy showing off your pretty moves while our own government keeps us prisoners!"

Pliés, battements, ronds de jambe, développés.

"When I get out of here," she storms, "I'm going to sue their asses off. I'll find me a tough lawyer who'll take my case on contingency, and I'll take on the entire rotten government! I'll make such a stink they'll regret they ever fucked with me!"

"They probably already regret saving your life," I said, turning to repeat my combinations with the other leg. "I know *I* do."

"Because all you care about is prancing around a stage in a fluffy tutu! Rucky-fucky dancer!"

"Philistine!"

"What does that mean?"

I can't help it; I laugh. It's not a happy laugh. Shana

Walders is the most abrasive person I've ever met. She's forced me to look at things I didn't want to ever see again, and she goes on forcing me now that we're safe. Because we *are* safe. This isn't some sadistic torture chamber where they cut up people or murder them or put their faces on chimpanzees. . . . But I won't think about that now. I refuse to think about that now. This is the Cunningham Federal Detention Center in Washington, D.C., where Shana and I are being temporarily kept safe until Dr. Nicholas Clementi can come talk to us. That's what we were told. We're in here for our own safety, and I for one am not unhappy about this, or wouldn't be if I knew that Rob wasn't worried sick about me and if the floor weren't concrete.

Shana says, "Don't laugh at me, Atuli."

"Then don't say stupid things." *Pliés, battements, ronds de jambe, développés.*

"You just don't react, do you? Whatever they do to you—cut off your balls, lock you up—you just take it."

She's trying to bait me. I lower my leg slowly in a *développé*—five, six, seven, eight—before saying, "I told you, it's not the same people who did both those things. Criminals tortured us. The government rescued us. Don't you even care about the difference?"

"The government screwed me!" she shouts. She's losing control; she really can't stand being confined. "Your precious government kept me out of the army in the first place because I just happened to see a bunch of monkeys with your face on them!"

There it is again. She won't let me forget. I turn to face in the other direction so I won't have to see her, even though I haven't worked the right leg enough. I raise the left. *Pliés, battements, ronds de jambe, développés.*

Shana charges across our cell and shoves the sofa hard enough to tip it over. It crashes down; I jump back just in time. "You stupid bitch! If that thing hit my knee—"

"Damn your knee! Atuli, don't *you* even care? It's not just all the little monkey Camerons! I told you what else I saw in that place. Some of those severed uteruses were made preggers with *your* sperm from *your* balls to grow *your* babies!"

She shudders; what she saw in the lab has shaken her in ways I don't claim to understand. Those aren't my babies, even if they use my genes. Sperm donors do that all the time. But she's said it again, the thing she just won't let me forget: the animals with my face. Out there. Acting like animals, drawing their lips back to show the animal teeth, grunting like animals, fouling their clothes or the floor, picking fleas off themselves and eating them, smelly and lumbering and mindless . . . with my face.

"Leave it alone, Shana! Just leave me alone!"

"I only wish I could, you rucky-fucky shit!"

I go in the bathroom and close the door, the only way I can get away from her. But even in the bathroom, I can't get away from the memory of the toddler standing beside me, staring at me with my eyes, chittering and horrifying and climbing the curtains with long curved hairy feet. . . .

I cover my face with my hands and lean against the bathroom wall.

But after a few moments of that, I straighten. The sink is only hip height to me, but the towel rack is higher, and it seems to be firmly fastened to the wall. I hold onto it and *plié.* There's not much room, I won't be able to do any *grand battements,* but at least I can stretch. And if Shana starts yelling at me through the door, I can always turn on the sink and shower and let the water drown her out.

He comes into the room slowly, leaning on a cane, and I realize he's at least partly blind. I didn't know that. It's the first time I've actually seen Dr. Nicholas Clementi.

"Hey, Nick," Shana says, and I glance at her in surprise. I didn't know her voice could have that softness in it. "Sit down here." On the sofa, which has been stood upright again, facing outward.

"Shana. Mr. Atuli," Dr. Clementi says, formally. He sinks into the sofa cushions and briefly closes his eyes. He's very weak. Yet he's here alone, the only person to come into our cell in a week and a half.

Shana says, "You look like shit, Nick. Didn't that French hospital help?"

"That French hospital saved my life," he says, and now he's looking at her with amusement. He's extremely old, but very well dressed, and he has a polished personal presentation. I can't imagine how someone like him and someone like Shana could like each other, but it looks like they do.

"Really?" she says. "You beat the sickness? Good for you. Now tell us what you're going to do for us, and why the fuck we're being kept here like some kind of criminals! I uncovered an illegal vivifacture lab, for Chrissake! Nobody don't seem to realize that! What the fuck is going on here?"

Again that look on Shana's face, that shudder. Dr. Clementi sees it, sitting so close to her. He takes her hand.

"Yes, you did uncover an illegal vivifacture lab. And a whole lot more. Shana, Mr. Atuli, I have a lot to tell you, and I can't talk for very long without tiring. So please stay quiet and let me say what I must, without interruption."

He doesn't move his weak old body on the sofa. But somehow it's as if he's gathering himself together for a major jump: a *grand jeté*, a *cabriole derrière*.

"Shana, I can get you accepted into the regular army. Cameron, you can return to Aldani House and dance in peace, at least for a while. But there's a price for both of those things, and this is it. Shana, you can't sue any-body, or—"

"How'd you know I been talking about suing?" Shana demands. "This jail is bugged? And you're part of it?"

"Yes to the first, no to the second. Be quiet and listen. You can't sue, and you can't sell your story to the press, and you can't ever blackmail anyone about this, even if you get tossed out of the army for the sort of totally unrelated insubordination I know you're capable of.

"Mr. Atuli, you'll have to live knowing that the vivifac-tured baby-substitutes with your face are out there. They won't be hunted down and destroyed, and eventually some reporter somewhere will see one and recognize it and it'll be all over the world media. After that happens, you'll no longer be able to just dance. Every time you set foot on a stage your audience will see not just your dancing but your monstrous notoriety, and you won't be able to tell them that it wasn't voluntary."

I manage to get out, "And if I don't agree to this . . . price?"

"The alternative is that the whole story be told right now, and you won't have even an uncertain interval of peaceful dancing before the media turn your every performance into a sideshow." The old man looks straight at me from his blind eyes. "I'm sorry, Cameron. They're not good choices."

"What *is* the whole story, Nick?" Shana demands. "And will they destroy . . . what I saw in the lab, with Cameron's—"

"Maybe. Maybe not. But you and I will never know either way. God, I'm tired. I came straight from the airport."

Despite my numbness, I'm surprised that he'd ask for pity like that. He doesn't seem the type. But then I see Shana squeeze his hand, her face softening again, and I realize why he did it.

"The trouble is," Dr. Clementi continues, "there are so few of you children now. You *are* a precious resource. When something is precious, everyone tries to protect it. Even from the truth. Nobody has told either of you the truth about what's happened to you, not since the day Cameron was kidnapped for his pan-ethnic beauty. I'm going to tell you the truth now. Yes, Shana, this room is undoubtedly bugged. But I'm going to tell you the truth anyway, and then the three of us will decide what to do about it. If our own government lets us."

Dr. Clementi pauses, and looks around slowly at the walls. I hold my breath; I think Shana does, too. But no one comes in. No one stops him.

And he tells us. He tells us what happened to me, and how, and why, and who let it happen. The same for Shana. I don't want to hear it, I want to rehearse in my mind instead, something like the lovely *pas de deux* from *Summer Storms: promenade* in *attitude*, finish with the lift . . . but I can't. I have to listen. Dr. Clementi tells us everything.

When he finishes, his body sags back against the sofa. Shana says, "Son of a bitch," and he smiles tiredly.

"To whom in particular are you referring, Shana?"

"All of them!"

"Not necessarily. At any rate, what we have to decide is—"

"I can see it for myself, Nick! Whether to go on pretending no kidnapping and castration and what-all don't even happen, or to blow the whistle!"

"And so end the research that might solve the endocrine-disrupter crisis," Dr. Clementi adds. "Don't forget that piece."

"Are you saying we should—"

"I'm not saying anything," Dr. Clementi says testily, and it's the first time I've heard him sound like an old man. "I'm *asking* you two, who are so intimately involved in all this, which choice you would make. Cameron?"

Shana says hotly, "Cam wants—"

"Let Cameron speak for himself."

"But he don't—"

"Shana. Let Cameron himself say what he wants."

"I just want to dance!"

Both of them look at me, and I know what their looks mean. I can't "just dance." There is no longer any way just to dance, to forget, to escape what happened to me. The three of us have to choose the best thing to do, so we have to consider our memories, all of them. That's the way it is. And not even dancing can make it any different for me, not ever again.

21

NICK CLEMENTI

It is a terrible thing to betray people who have trusted you. It's worse to do it in front of millions, on television.

Lights shone on the stage from both ahead and above. They were hot; the row of eminent scientists sitting on the stage started to sweat, small clear individual drops of water making their way through thin gray hair, down suit collars, onto conservative light lipstick. The lights were also blinding. I wasn't the only one on stage who wouldn't be able to distinguish faces in the packed hotel ballroom. But unlike the others, I knew who was out there, and where some of them sat.

Shana, in her new army dress uniform, would be in the second row. She would be sitting very straight, very solemn, very young. Sallie, reinstated at the CDC, sat with her husband and Maggie at the far left. Somewhere safely in the back were Cameron and Rob.

I had insisted, in the strongest possible terms, that these three groups arrive, and sit, and leave separately.

Out there, too, was the scientific press, buzzing with excitement. The popular press would look less eager. They were used to portentous announcements of "major scientific summit meetings." As far as they knew, this was just one more. A few reporters, however, the sharpest ones, would have the alert look of tigers that scent wounded prey. Those were the ones sitting in the back; if this press conference was what they suspected, they'd want to be able to rush out to interview manufacturing executives, robo-cams in hand. Stories are better with vids of first blood.

"—come together on this stage to make a singularly important announcement, in what well may be the singularly greatest gathering of scientific talent of all time," Vanderbilt Grant said from the podium, in his rich mellifluous voice, with his rich mellifluous exaggerations. Or perhaps not.

I sat at the far end of the row of chairs, almost in the wings. Beside me sat Eric Kinder, of Whitehead Biological Institute, a trusted friend. Eric had done spectacular work on hormonal brain differences between infant identical twins—differences that could only have been caused by prenatal influences, most of them negative. We had corresponded extensively. He had been on my side for years. I could see the flesh of his neck working up and down over his collar as he gazed down the long row of his colleagues.

Margaret Futina, National Institute of Health Neuroscience Center, who had hard evidence of synthetic chemicals' disruption of male Sertoli cells, those treasured producers of sperm. Her evidence had, somehow, never been published because, somehow, it "didn't meet peer-review standards."

Heinrich Feltz, Berlin Institute, who had done the most exhaustive study ever on the chemical contamination of breast milk, discovering 256 different synthetic chemicals—and then going on to do the first work on their interactions with each other inside the infant human body.

Wong Yue, Chinese People's Academy of Science, who

had perfected new methods of accurately measuring chemical concentrations in parts per trillion.

Marian Pearson, University of California at Irvine, who had used Murphy scanning to identify pinpoint brain malfunctions and cross-correlated them with selected chemical deposits in thyroid glands.

Albert Goldmann, University of Guelph, Canada, who had developed proof of falling sperm count due to endocrine disruption in mammals other than man.

Shoshona Ellinwood, Tufts University, whose work with pre-school children had found alarming nationwide increase in aggression and decrease in concentration—and correlated that with dose curves for synthetic pyrethoids.

Luigi Accorso, Medici Foundation of Rome, with research into how synthetic chemicals shut down human feedback mechanisms that were supposed to act as failsafes against endocrine-product overload.

Patrick James Sharpe, Harvard, whose research—much of it carried on against departmental opposition—linked selected synthetic disrupters to faulty manufacture of neurotransmitters in the brain.

"This illustrious gathering, this distinguished assembly," Vanderbilt Grant went on, and no one in the huge audience could tell from his demeanor how much he hated doing this "—will address the premier medical crisis of our time: the terrifying fall in birth rate throughout the world. And we will do so not in the ineffective ways of previous conferences, but with a bold new direction: a concentrated attack on the bioaccumulation of synthetic chemicals that may be disrupting the human endocrine system."

May be. Even now, Van was covering his ass. He stood at the podium, hands braced against it as if in a high wind, transfixing the cameras with the magnetic power that never left him. It hadn't even left him in the luxurious cell in the Cunningham Federal Detention Center where Shana, Cameron, and I had told him our decision.

"You can't, Nick! My God, do you have any idea of the economic results . . . consider. Consider carefully. Synthetic chemicals on your suspect list are found in everything, and I mean everything, produced and used in this country! Plastics, machine tooling, shampoos, fuels, food packaging, fertilizers, solvents. . . . The kind of serious government-sponsored scientific investigation you're talking about would . . . you'll get panic and hysteria over product use, massive changes in manufacturing requirements, bans and added costs. We can't take it, Nick. The economy is fragile already—it could collapse. Not just falter—collapse."

"And the current administration with it," I said. "Including you. Yes, I know. But that's the choice. If you let the real science get done—publicly and with establishment legitimacy—then Shana and Cameron and I will say nothing about the illegitimate branches of it you're condoning to get the DNA research."

"Yeah, that's the price," Shana brayed.

"That is our choice," Cameron said quietly, and threaded his hands together, and looked at his own dance-toughened feet.

"From time immemorial," Van intoned on stage, "what has been the first question of every civilization? It has been this: 'How fare the children?' When children flourish, so does the society. When children sicken and die, as they have in the great terrible plagues of history, the society loses heart and something in it also dies.

"That is where we stand now: not because our children

are dying, but because they are not being born. Without the next generation, this one is lost, unanchored, sickened in that part of us most fully human. No society can flourish that cannot look its own future in its small faces, tuck its own future into bed at night, see its own future in the shine of innocent young eyes. And that is why no price is too great for any exploration of the human tragedy upon us. No price at all!"

"I don't think you really know what you're asking," Van had said to me. "I don't think you understand what taking on the manufacture of synthetic chemicals will actually mean. And there's no hard evidence that it's even the cause, Nick—you know that. A dozen competing theories—"

"That's our choice," Shana repeated, with satisfaction. She was a child, enjoying a child's triumph—she, Shana Walders, was forcing the United States government to choose her way!

Van and I looked at each other. Old men, we both knew what was really happening here. There was no choice. If I had said, "No, Van, forget the bribes, we're going public with the evil you're covering up"—if I had said that, Shana and Cameron and I would never have left that prison. It might have been done quasi-legally: charges brought, no bail, matters of national security. Or it might have been done quasi-medically: psychosis-inducing drugs, one of us killed the other two, must never be set free, terrible tragedy, all recorded on camera. Or it might just have been done.

But from Van's point of view, keeping what I knew away from the press wouldn't have been easy anyway. Who else had I already told? Maggie, most certainly. What could he do about her? And who else? Van didn't know. He studied my face, while Shana grinned like the innocent she didn't think she was, and I saw him weighing the risk of silencing us against the risk of a government-backed exposé of the entire synthetic-chemical infrastructure of American materialism.

I saw the moment he decided.

After all, an exposé is only the first step. Action must follow, and action takes a long time when findings are as opposed as this was going to be, by as many powerful economic forces. If history showed nothing else, it showed that. Even if the conference proved conclusively, beyond all doubt, that synthetic endocrine disrupters were leading to the extinction of the human race— even if we proved all that, changing it would take time. A very lot of time. By which point, Vanderbilt Grant would probably be dead anyway.

It's the ultimate, perhaps the only, triumph of the old: we cannot be made to clean up the messes we leave behind.

"Okay, Nick," Van said softly. "You got your conference."

"Fucking right!" Shana cried.

"Over the next two years," Van said in his thrilling voice, "this blue-ribbon panel will devote a hundred percent of its time and energy to investigating two vital things: What are the causes of the population crisis? And how can we reverse those causes at their roots? These scientists will test theories connected to natural body cycles, environmental effects upon those cycles, prenatal influences, and infant nurture. No stone will be left unturned—"

He actually used that phrase. It was a measure of Van's tension. Usually he avoided both the trite and the comprehensive. His right hand, I saw by intense squinting, was in his pocket, where its trembling would not be recorded on vid.

"—in our search for answers. Practical answers that will

make a practical difference. And this administration
pledges its funding, to whatever extent is necessary, for
those two full years. You have President Combes's assurance of that, and my personal assurance as well."

"I want some assurances, Van," I said. "Here and now, on
camera."

Van nodded. Shana settled herself on a chair, looking expec-
tant. Cameron continued to gaze at his bare feet. For the first
time, I noticed the pattern of sweat stains and depressions in the
carpet of the cell. Barefoot, he had been dancing.

Van said, "What do you want?"

I said, "Anonymity for Cameron, complete and total."

Van snapped, "He would already have that if it hadn't been
for your girl here."

"Acceptance into the army for Shana. With your personal
written guarantee of no harassment or special scrutiny of her."

"Yes." He said it as if it physically hurt.

"Reinstatement at the CDC for my daughter Sallie."

"Certainly. I already told you that was a mistake."

More than that was a mistake. I didn't say it. "Complete autonomy for the scientific conference: in invitations, procedures,
televisation, conclusions, and publications."

"Yes."

"Government funding, at the Class Three level or better for
two years"

"Yes."

"Complete autonomy in choosing the panel members."

"But if you . . . oh, all right. Yes."

"Public acknowledgement, government security, and presidential endorsement of our findings."

"Nick, you know I can't—"

"Then at least you sponsor their presentation to the President. You, personally, as FDA head. And to Congress as well."

"I reserve the right to have others present contradictory findings at the same time. After all, there are always multiple ways to interpret data."

He would allow equal time to the manufacturing corporations, pharmaceutical companies, agricombines, everyone who used synthetic disrupters—which was indeed everyone, Van was right about that. Equal time even if the corporation-sponsored "findings" were misleading or bogus. But I knew I couldn't budge him on this; it was the way science itself worked. You were supposed to keep an open mind and consider all possibilities.

"Agreed," I said.

"Hey, Nick," Shana said, "Maybe you should lie down. You look wiped out."

She was right; I was exhausted. My neck throbbed. The base of my spine felt like old paper, crumbly and fragile. I needed to save my strength. Only I knew how much more it was going to be needed for.

"So I count it as a privilege to welcome this distinguished panel of scientists to Washington," Van said. From the back of the room a robocam detached itself and floated high over the stage for an aerial shot. "Speaking for this administration, we are sure that their work will make a tremendous difference to us all. That work represents an open-ended synergy of many different disciplines and theories. And we are pledged to receive their theories and recommendations in the same open-minded manner in which I know they will offer it."

Here it came. Open-ended. Open-minded. Theories. All the

buzzwords for "not conclusively proven." So that later, when the synthetics manufacturers offered their own theories that exonerated their products, Van could also champion them—if the wind blew that way.

As of course it would.

No matter. The conference would bring the issues into the open, would provide a solid scientific and moral foundation for the political fights to come. These scientists would do what they could to aid the side of objective truth.

Next Van introduced each panel member, who stood to receive applause. The scientists looked slightly abashed; they were not used to this kind of attention. And they had an innate respect for the order of things: first you did the work, then you received the attention. They weren't comfortable with the fact that the press usually did it the other way around.

"Finally," said Van, "I'd like to introduce the conference chair, Dr. Nicholas Clementi."

It was time.

"Dr. Clementi has a long and distinguished record, both as scientific researcher and as advisor to the legislative process. Most recently, he serves on the Congressional Advisors Committee for Medical Crises. Please join with me in welcoming the head of the Special Presidential Task Force on Bioaccumulation, Dr. Nicholas Clementi."

I rose. Van greeted me at the podium, taking both my hands warmly in his. I could feel the tremor in his right fingers. He had been fiercely opposed to letting me make a personal statement. "Premature," he'd said. Eric Kinder, when I had talked to him during the planning of the press release, had pointed out that I was unlikely to cloak the panel purpose in the same softened euphemisms that Van favored. Maggie had said Van just didn't want to share the spotlight. Sallie had said he needed to keep the press conference as short as possible; he was sicker than most people thought.

Whatever his reason, he was about to be proved right. He should not have let me speak.

> *If you would not be forgotten,*
> *As soon as you are dead and rotten,*
> *Either write things worth reading,*
> *Or do things worth the writing.*

Benjamin Franklin, the master of cunning and double-dealing.

I moved behind the podium and waited until Van had eased himself onto my chair, at the end of the row. The lights made a nimbus, obscuring any glimpse of the faces I couldn't have seen clearly anyway. Among them I imagined Shana, second row center, tensed in readiness.

"Thank you," I said. "I am honored to head this conference, which I regard as the most important thus far in our young century. The damage done by bioaccumulation of synthetic endocrine disrupters is an unimaginable enormity. Beside it, both human fumblings with DNA and human triumphs over cancer and heart disease look puny. If we have no children, then it hardly matters whether or not we alter our genetic heritage, or conquer our inherited diseases. Without identifying and correcting the population crisis, we *have* no future. Even if, as I firmly believe, the direct cause of that crisis is our promiscuous use of synthetic chemicals, plastics, and alloys.

"For generations, we have trusted that each new wave of science will correct the problems created by the wave before it. And to some extent, that has happened. Toxic wastes were corrected by toxin-eating bacteria. Environmental cancer can be cured by tissue-isolation techniques. World hunger has been greatly eased by laboratory-enhanced crops.

"However—letting technology cure the problems that technology created is *not* happening now. No profitable scientific spin-offs have appeared to increase the dangerously falling birth rate—and the host of other endocrine-related problems accompanying it. So we will have to set aside our wish that new technology might always obliterate old consequences. We will have to act directly upon root causes. We owe our children, and our children's children, that much."

I tightened my grip on the podium and allowed myself, for only a second, to close my eyes. This was it.

Et tu, Brute—

"And we owe our children something else, too. The future that this conference is designed to save will only have value if it offers those who come after us not just life, but a life worth having. Dr. Grant spoke a few minutes ago about 'the first question of every civilization: "How fare the children?" ' When its children don't flourish, Dr. Grant reminded us, a society loses heart and something in it also dies.

"But 'flourish' means more than simply to be alive and functioning. To flourish, children need a society that values truth, justice, and honor. So do adults. And nowhere do we need that more than in our government—because history has shown well that when the government passes a Tip-

ping Point of corruption, the society itself cannot long en-
dure."

I didn't turn around, but I knew what must be happening behind me. Van rising from his chair; Eric Kinder
pulling him firmly back down, half in the shadow at the
edge of the press lights.

"Ladies and gentlemen, listen to me. Please. *We are at
that biological Tipping Point.*"

If Van struggled, Eric would quietly force him offstage.
Two large men waited unobtrusively to escort him through
one of the capital's Tipping Point tunnels to a distant parking lot. Vanderbilt Grant would be excused from the rest
of the news conference on the grounds of ill health. Everyone in the audience would understand. So many of them
were old themselves.

I said, with as much intensity as I could get into my
voice, "Your government has consistently lied to you about
its DNA-level scientific research. Worse, it has condoned
evil—actual evil—in order to get around the regulations
which it has cynically passed and to which it has cynically
paid lip service for the gaining of votes."

Behind me the scientists, of whom only Eric Kinder had
been aware that this was coming, exclaimed in several languages. The audience buzzed. A few people, blurs haloed
by the glaring lights, rose to their feet, startled or angry or
voracious. Reporters started to shout out questions. One
man materialized at the base of my podium and tried to
climb on stage. Security hustled him away.

"Illegal genetic-engineering labs have experimented with
both vivifacture and DNA research." I had to raise my
voice to make it heard over the din; my throat ached. "That
is *not* new knowledge to some of us. What *is* new is that

top government officials—clear up to Vanderbilt Grant and perhaps higher—have knowingly allowed kidnapping, torture, and organ harvesting from innocent people so that this research could go on. They knew it, and didn't allow it to be stopped! And I can prove it!"

Reporters crowded the edge of the stage, all shouting. I held up my hand, both to quiet them and because I couldn't talk much more. Just three more sentences.

"Please . . . listen." Slowly the noise died. "Our only hope—hope for survival and justice—is to look at the truth. To uncover as much of it as we humanly can, and to flood what we uncover with maximum light. We might wish to preserve a more comforting dimness—but we can no longer afford to do so. What I have told you is fact. Many people know the story. Here is one it happened to personally." And Shana pushed her way onstage, escorted by the chief of security.

She stood very straight at the podium, her long blond hair tucked under her military cap. The bright lights glinted on the metal fittings of her dress uniform. Her young voice rang clear and strong.

"My name is Private Shana Walders, United States Army. Two months ago I was kidnapped for vivifacture, but what I know started long before that. Other people are going to talk to you about my story, but first I'm going to tell it to you myself as clear as I can."

I wobbled back to my seat at the end of the row. Van wasn't in it, and Eric Kinder had vanished. I listened to Shana, who was speaking slowly and grammatically (she'd been carefully rehearsed), but with a certain unseemly relish. Cameron Atuli would have been better, far more credible, but he wouldn't testify. Even now he and Rob were slipping unnoticed from the press conference, preserving his last chance to dance as a dancer, not a notorious victimized freak. I hadn't pressed him to speak. Enough had been taken from him already.

As Shana talked, I closed my eyes. Offstage the others were in place to confirm, all those older and more sober others who would give credibility to her wild story. But the story was hers, and it was right that she tell it first.

She was enjoying it, the little witch.

I thought of Van, being escorted to his car in the underground tunnels of the Tipping Point. He would hear the remainder of the press conference on vid, an electromagnetic bomb shattering the rest of his life. I thought of the days to come: the feverish reporters, grim CEOs, hysterical public, defensive FBI, outraged politicians scrambling to align themselves right. And the international repercussions: trade agreements violated, accords broken. Whole economies built on trade with the United States would collapse, and their shaky governments fall. There would be threats of war, and perhaps war itself. Chaos, as Van had said. Built on his old and suffering body, that had been my friend.

Better that than on the bodies of children.

I listened to Shana, and tried to imagine how the world would change now, until my eyes simply couldn't stay open anymore and gratefully I dozed off in my chair at the forgotten back corner of the stage.

22

SHANA WALDERS AND CAMERON ATULI

The reporters keep me talking for over an hour, with the lights and cameras, and I love every minute of it.

Me—Shana Walders—liar and thief. No fancy committee will ever call me those things again. I'm a hero who helped bust the illegal labs, and anybody who don't remember that isn't worth my spit. I'm Private Shana Walders, United States Army.

"Private Walders, one more question—"

"I think Private Walders has told us everything," one of the scientists says at my elbow, and sort of shoves me aside. I start to cut her down, but then I remember that heroes don't behave like that, so I nod and smile and walk off stage, my head high, and watch from the side. Security made sure no reporters don't get backstage. So now the reporters fire questions at this scientist woman.

"Dr. Futina, do you think the laws governing genetic experimentation need to be relaxed in order to allow research to proceed openly—instead of condoning it underground?"

"It's a complex issue," Dr. Futina begins, and I tune out. The good stuff is over. I look for Nick, but he must of left. He looked pretty weak there near the end.

I leave, too, and stroll around to the front of the building in case any reporters want to interview me some more.

But they're all inside, afraid of missing something. So I catch a cab back to the base.

In the barracks Jennie Malone and Georgia Kimmel are fighting over a hairbrush.

"It's mine, hole-breath! I just bought it yesterday!"

"Yeah, certainly. And the one you bought just happened to look exactly like mine."

"On! Give it to me!"

"I'll leave it to you in my will."

"Hey," I say casually, "I was just on TV."

"Uh-huh," Georgia says sarcastically, "and I'm a three-star general."

"I was! You can probably see it on the news tonight!"

Jennie says threateningly, "You got just one more chance to give me my brush, Georgia Kimmel. Just one."

I say, "I just brought down a government, for Chrissake!"

"All right, Georgia, I warned you!"

Jennie grabs for Georgia, who starts slugging. Stewdees, both of them. I march out of the barracks.

Two fairly young guys from Company B walk past, in civvies. "Hey, Private, you got leave? Want to go into town with us for some fun?"

They're not bad looking, although nothing to put on vid screens. Maybe a week ago I'd of gone. But now I don't want to. Getting drunk or reconfigured or laid just don't appeal to me. I say, "Can't. I was on TV today, and I still got some details to clear up."

"Oh? You on a sex channel?" And they laugh like the morons they are and go catch the train to town.

I mope around some more. An hour ago I was on top of

the world, and now I'm nothing. What the hell is wrong
with me? I can't figure it out, and I can't stand trying to figure it out, so after a while I go get on the train, too, but not
to go to the bars. Better than staying around here with this
bunch of hole-breaths who don't give a damn what's going
on in the world.

Nobody's home at Nick's. But there are reporters ringing
the house.

I stay back, chewing on my thumb and considering. I
could go up to them and just like that, they'd all want to
talk to me. I'm still in uniform. I could tell my story again,
to people who have the brains to see how important it is.
But suddenly I don't want to. I said it all at the press conference, and nothing is going to be no different if I say it all
again. For the first time, I realize why Nick isn't at home.
He don't want to talk to reporters any more today neither.

So he won't be at Sallie's in Atlanta, because the reporters will go there, too. And to Laurie's. He really won't
want them at Laurie's, now that she . . . So where *is* he?

Somewhere private, with the rest of his family.

I don't have to think long. When I lived at Nick's, I went
through all his deebees. He and Maggie own a cabin in the
Blue Ridge mountains in Virginia. Nick bought it during
the Tipping Point, and he put it in a different name. It was
supposed to be a safe hidey-hole or some such shit. I don't
remember the address, or even the town, but I do remember the name he put it under, because it's so weird: Muzio
Mercy. Finding the place would be an interesting challenge.

I start to feel a little better.

Public deebees of property, first. I'm no pro searcher,
but I can usually figure out how to get around in libraries.

I could use a public terminal. But not dressed like this—finding Nick is sort of an undercover game, so I shouldn't be conspicuous. Well, I can stop at a store and buy me some jeans. I got my pay. First, a public terminal. . . .

And those Company B soldiers think that "fun" is getting reconfigured and bothering people. What a bunch of kids.

They're out there. I don't know where, but I can sense them.

The evening following the press conference, I dance *Firebird* to Stravinsky's raucous music. The huge, overbearing *jetés* of my entrances soar so high that I seem to hang in the air, suspended, before I land. The audience gasps at my *entrechats*, when I leap straight up and beat my legs together front and back, three and even four times before landing, like some huge caged eagle. My exits are followed by crashing applause and standing ovations. No one knows it is all fueled by desperation.

A role usually danced by a woman, Mr. C. has re-envisioned the magical bird as male: muscular, energetic, restless. Mr. C. has also set the ballet in an anonymous modern city. The set is all holos of towering skyscrapers and rushing maglevs and blinking signs, all of which dim and still only when the Firebird is on stage. I wear a costume almost completely holo, with dazzling red and gold plumage and a mask that is at once alien bird and human wildness. The prince and princess are small people in modern dress, diminished by their surroundings. The idea is that the Firebird rescues them from more than the evil magician—he rescues them from the dehumanization of their own world, through the power of his older, more potent, and centered magic.

"Some of Stravinsky's works," a critic wrote long ago, "are designed as a means of escape from reality."

It's after midnight when I knock on the door of Nick's mountain cabin, and blacker out than I never thought possible. No lights—probably they're all asleep—no moon, no stars. I never saw such dark. The mountains are a whole other program.

The cabin sits by itself at the end of a dirt road. After I found out the county it was in, I took a train to the biggest town and rented a car. That was really expensive, but by this time nothing is going to stop me, including not having no driver's license. I slipped the man behind the counter fifty bucks. I could of got it for nothing, from the way he looked at my tits, but I wasn't in the mood for all that.

For an hour I taught myself to drive the car. Nothing to it. Machines don't bother me. Then I printed an area map off a terminal in a gas station, and drove up. And I do mean up. The cabin is halfway up a mountain, and if I'd of known how many roads just drop off to one side, I might not of come. Real freezy. But here I am. The air smells of pine trees, and a breeze blows leaves around my feet, though it's too dark to see them. I only found the cabin because the rental car had a flashlight. This is the butt end of no place.

Still . . . it's kind of nice.

I pound on the door, and after a while a porch light goes on and John opens the door. "Shana! What the—"

"Shana?" Maggie says. She's right behind her son, knotting a robe around her waist. She scowls. "What are you doing here, and at this hour?"

"Visiting," I say brightly. "Don't worry, Maggie, nobody's following me. I made sure of that. Where's Nick?"

"Sleeping. And I'm not going to wake him, either. He needs his rest."

Well, that's true, anyway. Even if Maggie's being bitchy about it. I say, "Aren't you going to ask me in? It's cold out here."

And even then both John and her hesitate before they step aside. You'd think rich people would have better manners.

"All right, come in," Maggie says. "But I'm warning you, Shana, any publicity seeking you're still after is not going to happen here. I don't know how you even found this place. It's a private family residence."

John adds, "And you're not family. However much you might impose."

For a minute it hurts, then I'm mad. Don't these people realize what I did for them? For the country? Nick's the only one of them with any class, and Nick is asleep. Also weak and old. I'm about to light into John and Maggie when I realize that even though Nick might be asleep, nobody else is. There's a cry from some back room, and then another, and then Laurie comes in carrying the baby.

It's the first time I've seen it.

Its face is all screwed up, red and yelling over Laurie's shoulder. She pats it on the back and jounces it up and down. The little thing is wearing a one-piece fuzzy yellow sleeper with feet. All I can see is its face and little fat fists.

John says sulkily, "Your knocking woke up Timmy."

"Sorry," I say, but I can't take my eyes off the baby.

"Poor little snookums," Laurie says, which is enough to make you throw up. But Laurie looks happy. Tired and pale, but still happy. I step closer to get a better look at the baby, yelling its head off.

Maggie steps in to block me. "Since you're here, Shana, I suppose you'll need to stay the rest of the night. I'll make up the sofa for you, which I'm afraid is all we have to offer. John, dear, get sheets and blankets from the storeroom."

John slopes off, still sulking. It don't look attractive on a man his age. Maggie stands between me and the baby, which Laurie is still patting on the back and jouncing up and down. It stops yelling.

Maggie says quietly, "What exactly are you doing here, Shana?"

It's a good question. I don't have no answer. Getting here was a challenge, something to do . . . but now that I did it, the thrill is gone. What do I really need to see Nick for, anyway? Our plans are all over. They worked, and Nick got going the investigations he wanted—both investigations, the chemical one and the crime one. And both of them in ways so public that now they can't be stopped. Our part is over, Nick and me. So just what *am* I doing here?

Besides getting depressed.

I let Maggie make up the sofa and I lay down on it. I close my eyes. Maggie stays up a bit, fussing at her grand-kid and watching me, but when I pretend to sleep she finally goes back to bed. I sit up. Across the room Laurie, little in a huge old wooden rocking chair, nurses the baby.

I blurt, "How come you can do that? You didn't get stuffed and give birth!"

Laurie laughs. "No. But there are artificial hormones to

turn on the lactation process. And my milk is going through a filter to remove the synthetic additives. See?"

I can't help myself, even though it makes my skin crawl. I have to see what she's nursing. I get off the sofa and look down at where the baby rests on her lap. There's some sort of device between her tit and the baby's mouth, with a glass bowl cupping her skin and a plastic nipple in the baby's mouth. In between is a sort of shallow box filled with wads of pinkish stuff that the baby's sucking makes the milk pass through.

The baby's eyes are closed, though its little mouth is working hard. Now that it's stopped yelling, I can see its features clear, and I know right away what's wrong with it.

It isn't what I thought.

"We've only had him three weeks," Laurie says softly, touching the baby's cheek, "and already I can't imagine life without him. He needs us so much."

"You're happy," I say, experimental-like.

"Oh, yes, so happy! I always wanted this. . . . I needed this. And look at him . . . isn't he *amazing?*"

She means it. I look at the baby, and I actually think *Maybe a chimp would be better.* I really think that. With a chimp, you wouldn't expect it to grow up, would you? You wouldn't expect it to learn to talk and read and get excited about going to grandma's, so you wouldn't be disappointed. But with a baby like this . . . does Laurie know this baby will never do any cute-kid things, not even the cute-kid things a chimp could do? That this baby probably won't even sit up, ever, or talk or walk or grow up into a son who does stuff to be proud of? Of course Laurie knows. If I know, she knows. She's seen the same pictures in the news, the flattened face and wide-set eyes and all the rest that goes with the almost-empty mind. The pictures are everywhere, because more and more of these babies are being born, with half their brains not working right. Or hardly not at all. It's due to the endocrine-disrupter synthetics, Nick says.

Most of those kids are aborted before birth. But not this one. And Laurie and John adopted him, because it's their only shot at becoming parents.

For the first time, I realize what those chimps with Cameron Atuli's face really mean.

Laurie says, "Do you want to hold him when he's done nursing?"

"No thanks," I say, real fast. "I don't much like any babies." Which is true. Even normal ones. Smelly demanding little blobs.

Laurie laughs. She's so gone on this kid she can't get offended. She glows with that kind of happiness you can't fake, the kind that goes down under tiredness and problems and everything else. I shake my head and go back to bed.

Just the same, I feel a little lost. Laurie at least knows what she wants.

The ballet is an enormous success. I take nine curtain calls. I bow beside Caroline, who is radiant and panting as she holds her flowers, sinking again and again into her *reverence*. We will go on to perform *Firebird* in Atlanta, New York, San Francisco, Tokyo, Rome, and London. And the more cities I dance in, the more famous I become, the greater the chance of my unmasking.

Because they *are* out there—the reporters digging deeper every day into "the story of the new century." They are exposing everything, writing about it endlessly. Digging into the horrors of the illegal vivifacturers and their monstrous research.

Digging into the extent of the governmental coverup, with its fascinating question: How high up did knowledge extend of the "conspiracy of criminal silence?"

Digging into the dangers of synthetic endocrine disrupters.

Digging into the specific events leading to Dr. Clementi's sensational news conference.

Digging into everything. Eventually they will come to the vivifactured chimps with my face, and after that they will come to me.

At intermission Rob, hovering in the wings, urges me to have my own face vivifactured into something different. Maybe I will. Except that I don't really believe that would stop the reporters for very long. They're inevitable, like death.

After they find me, I will never dance again as only a dancer. I will be a freak, not an artist. So I dance now, hurling myself across stage with a speed and power I never before possessed. Time is short, and I have to do with it what I can, even though there is no firm ground beneath my feet and I know that I am dancing on nothing but blowing air.

I try not to think of it. I try to empty my mind, to become nothing but the music, the steps, the rhythm, the Firebird.

While I can, I dance.

The next afternoon Nick and I go for a walk in the woods surrounding his cabin. He hobbles along, leaning on his stick. It's got a lot of medical stuff built right into it, sensory fields and alarm systems and emergency patches. I hold up his other arm. It isn't much of a walk, but at least it gets us away from the others. A hundred yards from the cabin we sit on a big tipped-over log in the fall sunshine. The mountains around us are bright with colored leaves: red and yellow and orange and brown and I don't know what all. Fall sure don't look like this in the city.

"So, what happens with you now, Nick?"

He smiles and holds tighter to the top of his stick. "Do you know, Shana, that's the first time I've ever heard you inquire into another person's future?"

"Yeah, well."

"Well what?" he says, twisting on the log to look at me, and even though he's half blind, I swear he can see deeper than people with all their sight.

"Well," I snap back, "answer my question! What happens with you now?"

He says cheerfully, "I go on living until something else wears out that medicine can't fix, and then I die."

"That's a hell of an attitude!" I say.

"It's exactly the right attitude. But for me, not for you. What happens next with *you*, Shana Walders?"

"Nothing, I guess."

"You mean that now you have what you wanted, acceptance into the army, there's nothing more to anticipate?"

I don't say nothing, just stare at the mountains. But Nick goes on needling.

"Aren't you supposed to be a precious natural resource? You've exploited that all your life, haven't you? Don't stop now."

"What's that supposed to mean?" Now I'm getting mad. What business is this of his? It's my life.

He says, "Have you thought about Officer Candidate School?"

I hoot. "Me? Come on, Nick! I barely got through high school! Besides, I don't want to be in charge of enforcing no fucking rules—I'm the one who breaks them!"

"Are you sure?" he says softly. "Are you really sure that's who you want to go being, Shana?"

And I don't have no answer. Georgia and Jennie, fighting over a stupid hairbrush like it's the center of the world . . . Teela and Dreamie, hassling rucky-fuckies for cheap thrills . . . the stewdees in Company B, thrilled over one more night of getting drunk and reconfigured and in trouble . . .

Nick says, "OCS would take you, even with your grades and your record. You're a hero at the moment, although I think you're smart enough to know that won't last. More to the point, the pool of candidates has shrunk alarmingly as the learning-disability curves have risen. You're healthy and you're smart, despite having spent a lifetime acting otherwise. They'd take you. You could be Lieutenant Walders."

Lieutenant Walders. With a real career. Real decisions and real choices and real challenges . . . I stand up so fast that the log rolls a little and Nick wobbles on it.

"Sorry, Nick. But we better get back."

"Certainly," he says. I help him up. A few slow steps in silence and then he says, "Think about it, Shana."

"Watch that branch, Nick. Don't trip."

"I'd write you a recommendation. You could do it, you know."

Lieutenant Walders.

I say, before I know I'm going to, "Is Laurie really okay with the baby? With *that* baby?"

"Laurie has scaled down her expectations. But yours need raising, Shana. Remember, anything we think we know about ourselves is very likely to be wrong." Suddenly Nick sounds like he's talking to himself instead of me, and anyway I'm already sick of the conversation. Life should be for living, not talking about. That's the trouble with people like Nick: talk and think and wallow in stuff. Instead of getting on with it.

Lieutenant Walders.

We hobble another ten yards, the leaves blowing in glorious colors and the air smelling like God just jumped out of bed and made the world this morning. A rabbit runs in front of us. Maggie opens the cabin door and comes out on the porch, hands on her hips, watching Nick with her face all soft. From behind her comes delicious smells of cooking, meat and apples and baking bread.

I say, "Nick . . ."

"You can ask your sergeant for an OCS application," he says. "Or access it online. And on your next leave, I'll help you with it."

"Yeah?" I squeeze his arm. For an old guy, he's always been all right.

" 'How fares the child,' " he murmurs.

"What?"

"Nothing. Walk faster, Shana. Maggie's waiting."

"She don't like me being here."

" 'Doesn't like,' " he says. Oh, God—now it starts. Correct grammar and correct manners and studying books. Officers don't sound like stewdees, and they don't act like it neither. Lieutenant Walders is going to have to become somebody better than I been. Is going to have to live up to challenges, and work hard, and all that shit. *Raise my expectations*, like Nick says. And I got a lifetime to do it in.

Suddenly, despite Maggie scowling at me from the porch, I feel really, really fine. The sun shines, and the wind blows, and I don't even care what chemicals it's blowing into my endocrines. We can fix it all. We always have.

I laugh, and Nick and I go inside to dinner.